SHE'S MISSING

A gripping psychological thriller with a shocking twist
By Ann-Marie Richards

She's Missing

Missing, Volume 3

Ann-Marie Richards

Published by Ann-Marie Richards, 2022.

ACKNOWLEDGEMENTS

Thank you, Father, for all my blessings. To my amazing family and friends for your love and support. To Anne, for your professional work on my manuscript.

Table of Contents

Books by Ann-Marie Richards

Missing Series – A collection of gripping psychological thrillers

Missing (A gripping psychological thriller with a shocking twist you won't see coming)

Missing Daughter (A gripping psychological thriller with a shocking twist)

She's Missing (A gripping psychological thriller with a shocking twist)

Domestic Psychological thriller series

The Rich Housewife (A gripping psychological thriller with a shocking twist)

The Pretend Wife (A gripping psychological thriller with a shocking twist)

She's Missing

Caitlyn's home-based catering business is a dream come true. She can be there for her three-year old daughter and her husband Sam. Everything seems perfect. Until...

Caitlyn's little three-year old daughter Katie goes missing.

She literally vanishes into thin air.

Who did this?

Was it someone close to Caitlyn?

Was it a customer?

Someone had been following Caitlyn. That much she knew.

And she would stop at nothing to get her little girl back.

Missing Series

Missing – Book 1

Missing Daughter – Book 2

She's Missing – Book 3

Chapter 1 – The Present

Caitlyn Reede piped the frosting over the second batch of cookies as she stood in the kitchen of her home. She then added the sprinkles to her design. Perfect. Her home-based catering business was a dream come true—even though she wasn't yet making enough to replace her old income, the important thing is that she could be there for her three-year old daughter, Katie, and her husband, Sam.

Her husband Sam had been uneasy about it at first, having a business from their home. But then she reassured him that she only worked with organizations and select clients, providing the freshest baked cookies and cupcakes for parties. She was surprised at how many people wanted this service. It was a niche she enjoyed. And her daughter Katie loved it even more.

She looked at all the benefits. Mostly, that she could watch her daughter Katie. Sure, she went to the daycare part time, especially when things were busy around the house with catering gigs and busy season. But it worked out just fine. Caitlyn was her own boss, so if Katie wasn't feeling well, she didn't have to go to the daycare. That way Katie could still see her friends and socialize with toddlers her own age a few days a week and she could spend time with mommy for the rest of the week. It was a win-win situation.

Not to mention they saved money. Caitlyn looked at profitability. The cost of running the business from home saved them a lot. They were already in a home and could expense ten percent of the mortgage interest and utilities. There was little in the way of overheads and they didn't have to worry about paying full fees for full time daycare which could wreak havoc on their living expenses. Katie went part time so the cost was more affordable.

Sam worked in insurance in the adjustment department. It paid okay, but with the cost of living going up, it wasn't like he was management, after income tax he came home with barely enough to thrive.

Still, her business had helped to pay some of the bills in the home. When they had Katie, they knew they would have to make some changes.

She'd posted pictures of her menu and baked goods with the delicious frosting from the secret recipe online and had gotten tons of likes and follows. She even had her own hashtag, anything to do with yummy cookies.

She used a post office box for mail, except for deliveries of supplies. And she did all the prep work in her kitchen at home and delivered her goods to events or shows. The busy fall season meant most people were indoors now and having fun gatherings like Thanksgiving, birthday parties, and of course, her busy season over the Christmas holidays where workplaces hosted parties for their staff or customers.

Caitlyn piped the frosting over her delicious chocolate gooey cookie that had been cooling on the rack. A familiar sharp pain in her lower back got to her and she paused placing her free hand on it hoping this would sooth it away.

"Back still bothering you?" Sam asked her.

"I'll be fine."

"You should really have it checked out you know."

"I know, but I've got a dozen orders to work on."

"Why don't you get some help?"

He was right, but with her little girl home half the time, she didn't just want any stranger in her home. It wasn't as if she had an office space or a storefront. She had to be careful whom they let into their home.

Caitlyn looked outside the window and saw a blue sedan sitting outside on the curb. It had been there since early this morning when she rose to start the oven and bake the first batch of cookies.

That's strange. She'd never seen it in the neighborhood before. How long had it been there?

Oak Street was a very cozy small street in their town. It wasn't very busy and she noticed each tree, each car parked outside, each neighbor's house.

"Mommy, look!" Katie said rushing into the kitchen. She had a lovely drawing.

"Oh, that is lovely, sweetie. Did you draw that house?"

"Yes," Katie said proudly and Caitlyn's heart melted like the chocolate filling in her home-made cookies.

Kate had soft brown curls framing her lovely chubby face and the cutest nose she'd ever seen. She was proud of her little girl. But she was most proud of her childlike wonderful spirit. When did people change? That laughter, that joy in her step as if no care in the world, as if everything was all right. And whenever she fell off her little bike, she'd get right back up as if nothing happened and brush herself off and move along. She didn't sit and whine or cry. She was a strong spirit, a wonderful daughter. And Caitlyn was so thankful the day she was born. She would do anything for her daughter. She would do anything to protect her, to keep her safe from harm, to make her happy, to raise her to be the best person she could be.

Katie then rushed back to her play area.

Sam finished drinking the last of his coffee and placed the cup in the sink. He then grabbed his briefcase and kissed Caitlyn on the cheek.

"Right, see you later then," Sam said.

"What time will you be back home?"

"I'll be working late tonight," he said, rubbing his stubble. He usually shaved but not this morning. It made him look handsome as hell. She loved that about him.

"It's one of our colleague's retirement party," he continued.

"Oh, did you mention it before?" Caitlyn didn't know about his plans. She thought they would be spending a lovely evening together as a family.

He looked at her, surprised. "Yes, I've mentioned it a few times."

"Sorry, I must have forgotten to write it down."

"Are you sure you're okay?" He looked concerned.

"Yes, I'm sure," Caitlyn said, her eyes then drawn to the window as she glanced out at the curb again. The car was still there. The windows were tinted. That always made her nervous whenever she saw a car with tinted windows that she couldn't see anything inside. She didn't know why but it just made her squeamish for some reason.

"How long has that car been there?" she asked him.

He turned around.

"What car?"

"That car, there on the curb across the street."

He craned his neck and shrugged. "Who knows, why?"

"I just think they've been there quite a while."

He grinned. "You know maybe they're waiting for someone."

"For two hours?"

"Look, I've got to run," he said, glancing at the screen of his smartphone. Did anyone look at their watch anymore or a clock? It seemed as if the smartphone had replaced so many functions. People whipped it out to take photos, record memos, check the time, set the alarm.

She grinned. She was glad to be living in this age of technology, but things had been so different in the past, according to her parents. Still, it made it possible to run her business from home over the Internet. What a great option for those who want to save on expenses while raising children. She loved to get out, of course. And she did mingle with people at events when she delivered her goods in person. But it was nice to not have to rush into work every single day. And to be able to take time off when you wanted to or if you needed to in order to take your child to the doctor's office or nurse their cold, or if you just wanted to listen to an audiobook or go the movies in the middle of the day to take a break from a busy work schedule.

Caitlyn would do anything to protect her lifestyle and her family.

An hour later, after she packaged up her cookies to deliver to a retirement home party, she turned around and gasped. There was a man at the door. She froze.

Chapter 2 – The Past

The orange leaves on the tree swayed with the October wind. Gusts of wind and rain swept across the land. It was a beautiful place. Quiet. Calm. Relaxing. Well, it would be relaxing if she were not imprisoned there.

She got up from the bed and went to the window, glancing outside. There was no one. She was lost. In the middle of nowhere. She didn't even know the name of the town. She was isolated. Away from everyone else.

She was bored. Bored out of her mind. She wanted contact. She wanted to see other people. How long did they think they could really keep her there. Were they afraid she would talk? Was this some sort of punishment?

She glanced at the headphones on the side table. Lovely. She had the expensive ones. So that she could listen to music and drown out the outside world. But she didn't want to drown the outside world out. She wanted to be a part of it. Her eyes scanned the land outside. It seemed to go on for miles and miles. There were other cabins nearby. The place was filled with glorious trees and mixtures of oranges, greens, yellows and brown leaves. She could inhale the country scent, the fresh air, unlike the city pollution. This was different. This was serene. This was hell for her right now. She should be grateful she at least had windows that could open and all this place to herself. Well, not quite. She was sure someone was standing guard downstairs. Her door was locked. Her window opened to let in fresh air but that didn't matter since she was on the third floor of the old house. Technically, the attic. A full attic. Spacious and clean. But it was still an attic. She wouldn't make it alive in one piece if she tried to make a run for it out the window.

She then turned around and glanced into the mirror behind her. Well, she was not all alone, was she?

She then made her way over to the closet and glanced inside. Well, at least they made sure she had enough clothes to wear. But it didn't really matter, did it? No one was there to see her attire. Except those people. They often came to check up on her once in a while to make sure she was okay. To make sure she was not feeling stressed or sick.

Just then a sound interrupted her thoughts and caused alarm to ring inside her.

"Who's there?" she called out. She then walked across the room, the old wooden floorboards creaking underneath her bare feet.

She leaned up against the door to her room. She listened. Was someone there? Was someone on the other side of the door? Was it her captor?

Chapter 3 – The Present

"Hello," Caitlyn said. "Can I help you?"

The man stood in the doorway. He was a middle-aged gentleman dressed in a blue suit and he wore black-rimmed glasses. She thought she'd seen him before. Then she realized where she'd seen him. He was across the street, helping to unload boxes from a moving truck.

"I'm so sorry to barge in like this," he said, feebly. "I...I...I'm your new neighbor from across the street." The man had a charming stutter.

Caitlyn's heart reached out to him. She remembered a childhood friend stuttered and she became protective of him when the bullies would make fun of him. Bullies could be cruel.

"Oh, right," Caitlyn said, warmly, "You just moved in across the street," she said. She'd almost regretted saying that now. Would he think she was a nosy neighbor who watched her neighbors while not even coming over to offer help or bring a welcome gift? Well, it wasn't as if she couldn't see his house. It was right across the street after all.

Sam and Caitlyn had planned to go over to say hello and welcome the new family to the neighborhood, or welcome the new couple, she wasn't sure if they had children. Even though he looked to be in his forties, he could still have young kids. Lots of couples started later these days.

"Yes, I just noticed that your door was wide open."

Sam probably forgot to close the door in tight. It was a windy day in October. The wind probably blew the door wide open. That happened sometimes.

"Thank you."

"And this is for you," he said, holding out a package.

"For me?"

"Yes, it was on your porch as well. We have to look out for each other you know, there are people stealing packages from front porches. They call 'em Porch Pirates."

She grinned and shook her head. It was a nervous grin. She'd heard about Porch Pirates on the news. Yes, he was right, they had to be careful these days.

"Thank you," she said.

"I'm Steve, by the way. My wife Mary is at work right now."

"Hi Steve. I'm Caitlyn, my husband Sam is at work too." They shook hands. After she'd spoken she'd almost regretted it. Why on earth did she trust this man? He could be a criminal for all she knew. She had to learn to stop believing everything people said. On the other hand, he was being neighborly. And it was good that neighbors could look out for each other, wasn't it? But she wished she hadn't told him that Sam was at work. Even though he'd just told her his wife was at work. Sam always told her to never let people know you were alone. Although technically she wasn't. Her daughter was in the playroom on her toy bike.

"Well, nice to meet you. I'll be off now. I was just on my way to work. Those smell delicious," he said.

"Thank you." Was he expecting her to offer him some? She normally would but they were for a client.

"I have a catering business."

"Nice. You work from home then?"

Oh, no. She shouldn't tell him that.

"Sometimes," she said. She really didn't want to talk too much about her business. She had to learn to stop divulging too much about herself.

After he'd left, she glanced outside the window and noticed that the car that was parked suspiciously across the street was gone.

Then...

She also noticed she couldn't hear her daughter.

"Katie," she called out, wiping her hand on her apron.

Sam had told her it would be nice to knock out the kitchen wall so that she could see when Katie was playing in the playroom or living room. That way they could turn their old home into a modern open concept area, so they wouldn't feel so closed in. She had told him it may not be a good idea since she worked out of her kitchen and it could be a bit messy. Besides, she'd always loved the idea of having some privacy. She felt so exposed with the open concept. There was no place to hide.

Speaking of hiding. Was her daughter playing hide and seek again?

"Katie," she called out again. This time, sensing something was wrong. Why was her daughter silent? She usually called out to her.

Where was her daughter?

Chapter 4 – The past

Her heart pounded hard inside her. She ran through the rooms of the house, frantic, searching, almost tripping on the steps. The crib was empty. The baby's crib was bare. Even the blankets had been stripped from the crib. Those beautifully designed blankets and mobile.

It was empty.

She was gone.

She's missing.

"Where is she?" she cried out, shrieking with fury. "Where is she? What have you done with her?" Tears streamed down her face.

The only sound she heard was the sound of her own voice, her cries, her pleading which went unnoticed.

Her hair was a mess, her mind was in turmoil. The only thing she ever wanted, was gone.

"What have you done with her?" She turned around to face the person responsible.

There was no reply.

"She's mine. Where is she? You were supposed to be looking after her. Why did you take her? Thief. Give her back to me."

Still no answer.

Why were they doing this to her? What had she ever done? How could they do this? She couldn't believe this was happening to her.

"She isn't yours," the cold voice sounded finally, the eyes pierced her soul as they stared at her with contempt.

"But I found her. She was abandoned. I saved her."

"She isn't yours. There's no such thing as finders' keepers when it comes to babies. You know that."

She knew what it was like to be abandoned. So she helped those who were also forgotten, cast away like nothing. She was taking great care of her, feeding her, buying clothes for her. Why were they doing this?

They didn't seem to mind when she "found" other things for them.

"What are you going to do with her? She was abandoned. She has no parents. I nursed her back. She was cold."

She knew why they were doing this. They were being spiteful. They were being cruel. But she would stop them. She would do everything in her power to stop them.

She was never going to let them get away with this.

Chapter 5 – The present

Caitlyn felt a panic attack coming on. She felt as if she was going to spin out of control and drop to the ground.

"Katie!" she called out again, looking around. Then she stopped. The room was spinning around her.

She rushed to the cupboard to pull out the pill bottle and take her pill. She then took a swig of water that was on the counter. She drew in a deep breath.

Before long, Caitlyn heard the giggles of her daughter and relief washed over her. She let out a breath she didn't know she was even holding.

Her body suddenly felt relaxed.

She ran to the next room again, the playroom that had been empty moments ago.

If she didn't have a hot stove on, she would allow her daughter to sit with her in the kitchen but Katie was so fidgety and would want to open cupboard doors and get into mischief. It wasn't safe for her to be in the kitchen while her mother was busy working filling orders. She'd planned to take her to the daycare soon, right after she finished boxing up this batch of cookies for the party at the retirement center.

"There you are, sweetie," Caitlyn beamed.

"Mommy," Katie said with a bright smile, her teeth spreading from cheek to cheek. Her little girl held up her tiny arms for a hug and rushed into Caitlyn's arms.

What would she do without her little girl? Katie was the apple of her eyes. The joy in her life.

Caitlyn was very protective over her daughter. She hoped her past would not catch up with her. She was better now. She was healed, wasn't she?

After her daughter went back to playing on her toy bike in the playroom, Caitlyn closed all the doors and made sure they were locked. She made sure the windows and doors were locked.

Caitlyn then ran back into the kitchen.

She reached into her apron.

She pulled out the wristwatch that had been on Steve's wrist earlier when she'd shaken his hand. She heaved a deep sigh of remorse. What was wrong with her? She was supposed to be getting better. She wanted to be better. She had so much to live for. So much to give.

Why did she do that? She had to return the watch. He'd barely even noticed when she slipped it off his wrist. It was something she'd learned to do when she was forced out of her home and forced to spend time on the street. She regretted that. There was no excuse for what she'd done in the past. Taking things to relieve her anxiety. A doctor had once told her that it may have been to do with childhood trauma. The therapist even told her that her compulsion could also hereditary—some neurotransmitter abnormality. They were not sure though. It was just a theory but she had been in therapy to help her. She was fighting to be normal again. To beat the odds. She wasn't going back to that life. Never again.

In fact, that was how she'd met her husband Sam. She'd taken something off his windshield and he'd stopped her. She was so apologetic and he'd forgiven her and taking her out for coffee. The rest was history. He'd told her that everyone had problems. Though theft could land one in jail and it was best to get help as soon as possible. Come clean.

What would he say if he found out she'd slipped again. Her neighbor had made her nervous and she did the wrong thing. But she was going to make it right. She always did. She always returned what didn't belong to her.

She thought about her sweet daughter, Katie, and a wave of guilt rushed over her again. Well, there were some things she would *never* return.

Besides the obvious, she had to stop taking things that didn't belong to her. She had a problem. Caitlyn had a serious problem. She was getting better. But she had to stop now. This could ruin everything she'd worked so hard for.

Should she tell Sam what she'd done? But then what if he left her? She couldn't risk that. But she wanted to return the watch. Her impulse to take things had scarred her in the past and caused her to lose those close to her. She wanted help. Silently she pleaded for help.

She looked at her daughter, peeking over the corner with a sweet little mischievous grin on her lips. It was as if she'd sensed her mommy was quiet and thinking.

Caitlyn smiled back warmly. Katie then went back to the playroom and giggled and played with her toys. Caitlyn was going to take her to the daycare soon while she delivered her batch of cookies to her new gig.

Caitlyn then made her way to the pantry and opened up the fake back wall. She pulled out a steel box and opened it. There were several news articles in there and a diary notebook. Her secret was safe. The headlines were scandalous.

Baby Missing
Baby Kidnapped from Restaurant Police Looking for Witnesses
Scandal-ridden small-town mayor and his wife search for their daughter

Yes, there were some things Caitlyn would never return because it would kill her if she did.

Chapter 6 – The present

A light tapping on the door distracted her thoughts and caused her to jolt. It was her friend, Tiffany.

"Hey Tiff," Caitlyn said.

"Girl, what happened to you?"

"What?"

"You look as if you've been crying?"

Caitlyn wiped her eyes and glanced in the mirror stuck on the kitchen fridge.

"Oh, it's nothing. Just peeled some onions," she lied.

"Onions?" Tiffany looked dubious.

"Just kidding," Caitlyn said.

"Ah, good," Tiffany pulled one of her adorable funny faces, "because I was about to say, you should probably not be baking any more cookies if onions are one of the ingredients you use."

They both burst out into laughter. Trust good ole Tiffany to break any ice. She was glad to have her as a friend. Tiff was more like a sister.

Her friend came over to help her with the delivery. Tiffany was like her own family. Caitlyn wasn't close to her own, neither was Tiffany. They had that in common.

In fact, Tiffany once told Caitlyn that she'd had a traumatic childhood and early adulthood.

Strangely, Tiffany never did elaborate beyond that. She'd just told Caitlyn that her life was so messed up she'd rather forget it.

Caitlyn could certainly relate to that. She never had a conventional upbringing either. Not in her eyes, anyway. Not if conventional meant having a close-knit loving family that looked out for you and your best interests.

And Sam never judged her for not being close to her family and for that she was grateful. He, on the other hand, had enough family for both of them. In fact, they were supposed to head over to his mother's home later for dinner and his aunt's birthday party at the same house.

She only wanted to be a better parent to her daughter than she'd had. Was that too much to ask? She vowed she would be the best parent and give her daughter everything she never had when she was growing up. She was going to give her love, time, attention, guidance and nurture. Everything so that she could flourish in this unpredictable world and be strong and get help if she ever needed. To be a giver, not a taker in life.

"Okay, I guess we can get these boxes into the car," Caitlyn said.

"You want to take my car? My SUV has more space."

"Sure, why not?"

After they'd finished getting the boxes of cookies into Tiff's SUV, Caitlyn turned back to the house to get her daughter.

"Okay, sweetie, time to go to the daycare for the afternoon," Caitlyn said in a sing-song voice.

"Mommy," Katie said and clapped her hands together. "Daycare."

"Yes, that's right. Daycare. You're going to have fun playing with all your friends while mommy gets these treats for her client."

"Okay, Mommy."

Caitlyn smiled warmly as she grabbed Katie's pink-colored backpack and scooped her daughter up in her arms.

She knew Katie was quite capable of walking to the SUV but she often had a tendency to run off. She loved to run. Caitlyn always worried about her running off while going on an excursion with the daycare. Most of the early childhood educators had a few children in each of their care. Would they watch her carefully? Katie had a ball of energy for a little three-year-old. Still, Caitlyn knew deep down the daycare staff knew how to do their job well. She was just grateful for the option to have her daughter attend part-time. It was all she and Sam could afford right now.

"That was a good turn out," Tiff said later that afternoon to Caitlyn, offering encouragement. They both sat in a coffee shop after her catering gig earlier in the day.

Caitlyn needed encouragement. After all, it wasn't that great of a turnout. A few of the residents had been sick with a stomach bug. And another resident had gotten confused and smashed a few cookies over another resident's table.

But Caitlyn was glad for any catering gig she got. Thank goodness for dear Tiff who helped her clean everything up. She was hoping for some referrals but the staff were so busy tending to the other residents. There were a few that were very happy to see them and another asked if she could bake cookies for their granddaughter's birthday party, so that was good.

"Thanks. And thank you so much for helping me out there."

"Hey, it was my pleasure."

"What would I do without you, Tiff?"

"Same here. You've been a good friend, Caitlyn." She smiled.

"There's nothing like a nice warm mug of Pumpkin Spice Latte," Caitlyn said.

"Here, here."

They both held up their drinks and clinked the cups.

The taste of the smooth, rich creamy latte soothed her throat as it slid down warmly on this chilly October day.

Caitlyn also called the daycare to check to see how Katie was doing. She always kept tabs on her little girl. Her precious little earth angel. A gift. Katie was so happy with Caitlyn. She remembered when she taught Katie to call her mommy. It was such a wonderful sound to her ears to hear that. Katie only had memories of Caitlyn being her mommy. That was all that mattered.

When she'd gotten off the phone, she noticed Tiff was busy scrolling down her phone and then typing something in, probably sending a message. She didn't even notice when Caitlyn had finished her phone conversation.

As her friend ferociously typed away on her phone, moving her finger fast across the screen, Caitlyn looked around.

When she looked out the window, her heart stopped.

No.

Chapter 7 – The Present

"You look as if you've seen a ghost," Tiff said to Caitlyn.

Caitlyn then turned her attention back to her friend. "Sorry, it's just that. That car outside the window there, parked across the street. It was there at my house this morning."

Tiff looked outside the window. "Which car? There are a lot of cars out there."

Caitlyn swallowed hard. Uneasiness slid through her body. She wasn't seeing things. She knew she couldn't be seeing things. That's the trouble when you were on the run from your past. You never knew when it would catch up to you, if it did. You were always looking over your shoulder. Wondering. Caitlyn hated that feeling. She hated feeling as if she were being watched every waking moment of her day, of her life.

"I...I have to call the daycare again."

"You just spoke with them, didn't you?" Tiff gave her a worried look.

"I know, I just...they're supposed to be going on a school trip today. I just want to remind them to watch her carefully."

"You really worry about her, don't you?"

"Of course, I do," Caitlyn said, while waiting for the daycare to pick up. They probably thought she was one worrying parent. But she didn't care. Her daughter was her whole life. She was everything to Caitlyn.

Just then Caitlyn glanced around the café and she noticed most people were in conversation with each other but there was one man in the far corner directly in her view that wore sunglasses on—on this cloudy day with no sun visible in the sky. Was he watching her? He had a cup of latte in front of him, still full from what she could see. He was reading a newspaper. How convenient that he suddenly held the paper up to cover his face. Most people read from their phone or tablet, but he was reading from an actual newspaper. And she thought she caught him glimpsing over the paper in her direction. Had he been listening to their conversation?

"Caitlyn, are you sure you're all right?" Tiff asked.

"I'm sure. Let's go." Heat rushed through Caitlyn. Was she going to have another panic attack? She still hadn't returned the neighbor's watch. She had to do that later. She had to tell Sam what she had done too. She wouldn't tell Tiff though. The last thing she would want was for her friend to judge her or stay away from her. She was, after all, the only close friend she had right now.

Chapter 8 – The past

"Your daughter has a problem," the woman said. "She steals things. She needs to be put away." The voice was fierce and menacing. Devoid of any human emotion.

She watched as they both discussed her life.

"She kidnapped our baby."

"And she stole the Johnson's family puppy too," the other person said, acid in their tone. Their tone was so cold, it caused her to shiver for a second. It was as if the atmosphere around them was chillier in the room than outside on this cold fall day.

Fire burned inside her. They were not treating their dog very well; she only took the dog in to care for him. She would never hurt anyone or anything. She knew what that felt like. Some people just didn't know how to care for their loved ones. They didn't care about their dog, she did. She nurtured him and played with him. That was who she was. That was what she did. Why couldn't they see that? She never hurt anyone or anything. Okay, she did steal things. And that was wrong. But she did it for a noble cause. She was hurt. So she healed those who were hurt or neglected. It was her way of dealing with her own troubles.

The other person paced nervously. "She didn't know what she was doing. I...I'm sorry." The other person spoke but it was as if the words didn't register to her. "She's just a child. It won't happen again."

"It better not. I know all about you. She should be put away."

She knew as she listened she would have to make a move. She would have to runaway somewhere and go far away. She would have to change her name. She would be somebody else. Because there was no way she was going to let them lock her away somewhere. No way in hell.

Chapter 9 – The Present

The following Saturday, Caitlyn got Katie ready for the party over at her mother-in-law's house. They were going to be other kids there too, so she didn't bother hire a babysitter or take up Tiffany's offer to babysit her. She really didn't want to take advantage. Her friend Tiff had a kind heart and always wanted to help out. But Caitlyn knew she had her own life too.

Sam seemed pre-occupied on the phone in the study, while Caitlyn finished getting Katie ready. She wore her pink dress with a Dora logo. It was her favorite. She loved to dress her daughter in cute little outfits from her favorite TV characters. She didn't care what people said about toddlers and their energy level, it was fun for Caitlyn. It gave her a time to revisit being a child, carefree, always laughing, always having fun. That was how all children's childhoods should be.

Caitlyn also grabbed Katie's favorite bright yellow raincoat. The sky was overcast and the forecast called for light drizzle or rain later in the day.

Katie adored her yellow raincoat. Yellow was Caitlyn and Katie's favorite color. As mother and daughter, they shared a lot in common, even though Katie was only three-going-on-four or going-on-fourteen, depending on her day. As a mom, she loved when her daughter wore bright clothes, it not only lit up her face, but it made it more noticeable for her in a crowd. Not that she would ever be in a crowd.

Katie would often go out on day trips with the daycare, so Caitlyn wanted to make sure the teachers could always notice the kid in the bright yellow jacket. Yellow was a mood-enhancer too. At least that's what Caitlyn learned in her therapy classes. It brightened up her mood instantly and warmth and happiness slid inside her. It was called chromotherapy or color therapy and the belief was that color could balance energy in the human body. According to Caitlyn's chromotherapy workshop leader, green was the color of nature, yellow could elevate one's mood and orange created a feeling off warmth and happiness.

Maybe it was all psychological but color-therapy was a thing now. Of course, her husband and many of her associates called it total and utter crap, but Caitlyn didn't think so.

Having grown up in a household where her parents fought often while portraying another image to the public was daunting. Not to mention they rarely spent time with her. It was as if she was always invisible to her parents. As if she were just a prop for their image, not a real child. She could never get their attention. She vowed to never be that parent. She had tried everything to be loved, to feel wanted, to fit in to her parent's expectations, to not disappoint them. But nothing she did was ever good enough for them. She wasn't smart enough in school or dressed the way other girls dressed. She wasn't what they wanted.

She vowed to accept her own child unconditionally, to shower her child with lots of love and time and warmth. The idea of having a close-knit and supportive family was everything to her and she was glad now that she had one of her own.

Deep down Caitlyn knew there was something off about her parents, but she couldn't quite place what. She knew they were hiding something from her. Something dark and dangerous. She was glad she never stuck around to find out what it was. Maybe if she knew what they were really about, she would have been more damaged than she already was.

"Okay," Caitlyn said, cheerfully, "are you ready, sweetie?"

"Yes, Mommy. Toy," she pointed out to her big doll.

"Are you sure you want to bring that, sweetie. You might lose it." Caitlyn didn't mind her playing with the other kids, Sam's nieces and nephews, but they could be a handful at times and she knew she shouldn't be the one to talk, but they always seemed to abscond with Katie's toys whenever she was around them, playing. Katie would always be missing something.

"Knock, knock," Caitlyn said cheerfully before entering Sam's office space. She hated to just barge in on him in case he was on a Zoom call with clients.

She didn't wait for an answer and quietly opened the door and surprise took her.

Tiffany was sitting on the desk.

"Oh, I didn't know you were in here," Caitlyn said. "I thought you were home." Her surprise now turned to concern. What the hell was she doing in her husband's study?

"Oh, I was just stopping by to bring a punch bowl." Tiff didn't look at Caitlyn.

That was pretty casual of her to sit on Sam's desk. They must have noticed Caitlyn's startled expression. Heat rushed through her. What was her husband and her best friend doing in his study with the door closed?

Sam hesitated before stumbling with his words. He never did that.

"I...uh...I asked Tiff to bring a punch bowl over. Mom's bowl had cracked. She needed a new one."

"Oh,' Caitlyn said, not convinced. "Okay." She *wasn't* okay. But she just didn't want to start an argument right now. Not when she was about to visit her mother-in-law. Sam's mother was a nice lady and she loved Katie more than anything in this world. But she was also a powerful woman in the community with big connections and an even bigger mouth. Boy, did she talk about anything that was bothering her. And she loved to gossip, even about her daughters-in-law.

Caitlyn felt her skin prickle behind her neck. She sucked in a deep breath.

She then observed Sam and Tiffany. Tiffany slid herself off the desk after sitting casually with her legs crossed, dangling over the desk.

What was going on? Was it Caitlyn's imagination? Probably it was nothing. Yes, Tiff was still single. She'd once told Caitlyn that her fiancé broke off her engagement to marry someone else. She never spoke about who he was or what he did for a living. She was always secretive about that. She did tell her though that she'd planned to get him back one day.

Caitlyn didn't think it was a good idea and had told her she was better off without him. She'd told Tiff that she should just move on and stop living in the past. They never spoke much about the subject after that. Because whenever they went out to clubs or a bar and Caitlyn tried to play matchmaker for Tiff, Tiff brushed it off and told her she was not interested in dating for now.

Well, Tiff certainly looked as if she was in the mood to date now.

Stop that, Caitlyn. Tiff is your best friend. She's your only good friend.

That was true. Tiff was her only close friend and knew most, not all, of her secrets. But she should know better. She shouldn't be chatting with Caitlyn's husband in his office with the door closed. Not after all those lunches when she'd confide in Tiff about any little naggings she had about her husband. Not personal things, mind you, just small things like him not coming home early from work. Caitlyn would never divulge intimate details about her husband—ever. Whatever intimate things went on between spouses should be between them—unless of course, abuse or violence occurred. Then it was everybody's business.

"So, where's the punch bowl then?" Caitlyn asked.

Tiff said nothing for a moment. Both her husband and her best friend gave each other a funny look.

"I'd better get it out of my car. I'll be right back," Tiff said and left the room, a shadow of guilt spread across her face.

She'd be back? She'd better not be, Caitlyn thought to herself.

She then sucked in a deep sigh.

"I need to speak with you," Caitlyn said.

"About?" Sam said, turning his attention back to his laptop propped on his desk.

He didn't even meet her gaze. Why wouldn't he look her in the eyes? One thing she knew about her husband was that he was a terrible liar. He could never look her in the eyes if he were telling a fib.

"What were you two doing in here?" she asked.

He turned around and gave her a curious gaze. "What do you mean? We already told you. Mom's serving plate broke and she needed another one."

"I thought it was her punch bowl."

His body stiffened; his expression turned blank.

"Well?"

"Punch bowl, serving plate. Same thing." He turned his back on her again.

'No, it's not the same thing. What's going on, Sam. Are you cheating on me?"

"What?" Anger flashed in his eyes as he spun around to face Caitlyn. "Of course not. You know I would never do that." He looked her in the eyes this time.

"It's just that..."

"Listen," he said, "if you must know, we were planning a surprise for you."

"A surprise?"

"Yes, for your birthday?"

Caitlyn's stomach dropped. Of course. Her birthday was coming up soon. So they were planning something for her.

"I...I'm sorry, Sam. It's just that...well, things have been crazy lately."

"Listen, don't worry about it. Just don't tell Tiff, okay? She had this great thing planned for you. I'm not going to tell you what it is. You'll soon find out."

She felt relieved for just one second. Her brain went over the words he'd just used. He called her friend Tiffany by her pet name, Tiff. The one that Caitlyn used. Since when did he call her Tiff? He'd always called her Tiffany—until now.

Right now, Caitlyn was confused and didn't know what to believe.

Chapter 10 – The Past

She had to run fast. She had to get away. She was going to change. She was going to become someone else. Move to a new state, change her name. The first thing she would do was to erase everyone in her contact list. She was a new person now. The past didn't matter. The past couldn't hold her back, keep her down or catch up to her. She would make sure of it.

Chapter 11 – The Present

"Darling, you look lovely," Elaine Reede, Caitlyn's mother-in-law said as they walked up to the door. She was referring to Katie, her granddaughter.

"Hi Grandma," Katie said.

Just then, Lynn, the Reede's housekeeper came with her cheerful smile. "Would you like me to take your coat, Young Miss Reede?" she said.

Caitlyn smiled. She loved to see her daughter treated like a princess. Like the princess she was.

"Thank you," Katie said as the woman took her coat.

"Actually, she might need it later. It looks like it's going to rain and the kids are playing outside."

"Good call," Elaine agreed.

Lynn then held unto the coat. "Why don't I hold it for you and I will give it to you when you go outside," Lynn said, warmly.

"Okay," Katie said. She then pulled out her doll. "Toy," she then said, proudly holding up her doll to show her grandmother.

"Yes, it is lovely. Just like you. Would you like to play in the garden now or later?"

"Now," Katie said, happily as Caitlyn watched on smiling.

"Good, Riley will take you outside. The other kids are playing out there." Elaine then motioned for Lynn to put Katie's coat back on.

Caitlyn loved to see her little girl in joyful spirits. She was such a bundle of joy. Always happy.

In fact, she was the only happy spirit in the car as they drove over to the east side of town where his mother lived in her east coast mansion. Both Sam and Caitlyn were quiet throughout. She never did get a chance to tell him what happened when the neighbor came over to visit.

But it didn't really matter now. Caitlyn had corrected it. She'd gone over to her new neighbor, Steve's, house and told him that she found his watch. He had given her a suspicious look at first but then he said he didn't know it was missing and thanked her. How could he have not known it was missing? Didn't he try to check the time?

Then again, most people glanced at the watch on their smartphone these days to check what time it was. Still, he was grateful. And she didn't tell a big whopper of a lie, exactly. She told him she had found it—she just didn't tell him she'd found it in her hand when she slipped it off him. She had to be more careful next time. She had to learn how to keep her emotions in check. Her illness at bay.

Her medication helped her somewhat for her anxiety that led her to her behavior but she still had to be very careful not to slip. She'd vowed after Katie; she would never steal again. And she wanted so desperately to keep that promise she'd silently made to herself all those years ago. But would she be able to keep it? If she didn't, and she was caught and they found out about her little problem, she knew full well, she could lose it all. And that was something that was unthinkable.

Just then Katie's older cousin Riley came to hold her hand and the two of them went outside with scores of other children to play in the massive garden—if one could call it that. It looked more like a public park with its huge size and impressive landscape.

Caitlyn was so glad her daughter had kids her age to have fun with.

"So how is business?" Elaine asked Caitlyn later in the grand kitchen. Elaine played with a pearl necklace around her neck as Caitlyn spoke. The woman loved to fidget with her jewels, Caitlyn noticed. She wondered if she did this when she was bored or didn't really want to know the answer to the question she was asking. She was dressed in a lovely silk dress and her hair was done up in a perfect coif. In fact, she looked flawless from head to toe. There wasn't a hair out of place on Elaine's head. Unlike Caitlyn who wore her hair in a messy bun sometimes. It was always more comfortable, but she would often catch the disapproving look of her mother-in-law.

Still, Sam didn't mind one bit. He'd told Caitlyn he loved the way she did her hair. What she hated though was whenever Elaine criticized how she did Katie's hair or how she dressed her little girl. Thankfully, Elaine didn't make any comments today. Which was unusual since she often made an off-handed joke about it. But many truths are spoken in jests, as the old saying went.

"Oh, it's good, thanks," she said, then she noticed a huge spread of desserts on the table. There were pies, cupcakes, cakes and...cookies.

Caitlyn's stomach fell.

"Oh, you have large chocolate chip cookies," Caitlyn commented, trying to sound cheerful.

Elaine suddenly looked guilty. "Yes, we decided to have them catered in."

Caitlyn's stomach tightened into knots. "Why didn't you ask me? I could have whipped up a batch. You know that's my specialty."

And she could have really used the gig. She was building up her business. Did Elaine seriously pay a competitor to cater the desserts for the party instead of her own daughter-in-law? When Caitlyn had asked a while ago if she could bring anything or cater for the party, Elaine had said no. She'd even told Caitlyn they would not be needing any desserts since they already had the birthday cake and children didn't need any more sugar in their system. That was her words.

She noticed Elaine swallowed hard, probably fishing for an excuse. But it was no use. Right now, Caitlyn didn't really care. Well, that wasn't entirely true. She did care. She cared a lot. Elaine was her mother-in-law. She had powerful friends, prospective clientele for Caitlyn. Why on earth didn't she take Caitlyn up on the offer? Didn't she like her offerings? Caitlyn had been getting lots of great reviews on Google for her new enterprise. She would have really appreciated it.

"Is everything okay in here?" Sam asked, walking into the kitchen with a beer in his hand.

"Yes, everything is fine, darling," his mother said. She was then distracted by a friend and excused herself to talk to her guest.

"Well, I'm really surprised," Caitlyn said to her husband after his mother had left the kitchen.

"About what?" he asked, taking another swig of his beer.

"This," she said, gesturing at the spread on the kitchen island. "I asked Elaine if she needed any refreshments for the party and she said she wouldn't need any cookies because the kids would have cake and that was enough."

He shrugged. "Maybe she changed her mind."

"Yes, but why didn't she ask me? I would have loved to have done it. You know I'm building up my portfolio for my Instagram. The more gigs, the better."

He heaved a sigh. "It's no big deal, babe," he said. He then leaned over and gave her a peck on the cheek, smelling of alcohol mixed with cologne.

Something then struck her. Why was he wearing his sexy cologne? He only wore it on special occasion. He had it on at the house too when he was alone in the study with her friend Tiffany, who by the way, was also at the party—talking to another friend.

Tiffany had always been at the house whenever there was a party for Katie, so she'd ended up speaking with Sam's mother a lot. After all, Tiffany was the godmother. She never had kids of her own but she loved kids and was good with them.

When Tiffany came into the kitchen Sam gave Caitlyn another peck on the cheek and made his way out without even looking at Tiffany. Was it because he didn't want another confrontation with Caitlyn again or was it something else?

"You look worried," Tiffany commented. "Everything all right?"

"Why is everyone asking me that?" Caitlyn shook her head. "I'm fine."

Caitlyn was going to mention the idea that cookies were being catered at the party and she wasn't even asked by her own mother-in-law but she decided not to bother. She would just let it go.

She glanced out the kitchen window to see how Katie was doing. Her daughter was happily playing with her older cousins and some other kids. They seemed to be having a ball outside. That warmed her heart. It was good that she was using up a lot of energy. That meant that she would have a good night sleep tonight which made it easy for Caitlyn as she had to work late tonight on her marketing materials for her Instagram page and YouTube channel.

Just then Riley came rushing in the kitchen and bumped into Tiffany.

"Oh, no." Tiff looked in horror as she glanced down at her neatly pressed white blouse. It was drenched with red juice.

"Shit!" she said. "Why don't you watch where you're going," Tiff yelled at Riley. Caitlyn was startled. She'd never heard Tiff shout like that. It was an accident after all.

"Here," Caitlyn said. "Let me clean that for you," she said, grabbing a sheet of paper towel from the counter.

"It's ruined," she said, slamming her cup down on the kitchen island.

"It'll be all right. It's only punch and water. It'll wash out."

Tiff lifted her top slightly and Caitlyn gasped.

Her midriff was showing. All these years she'd been a friend of Tiff and she'd never seen her midriff. It was filled with stretch marks!

The kind of stretch marks one got when you've been pregnant.

But Tiffany said she'd never had any children.

Caitlyn looked away hoping Tiff didn't see her gasp.

Elaine then came into the kitchen. "What happened to you?"

"Nothing, Riley bumped into me. It's just a little accident," Tiff laughed it off lightheartedly. By then Riley had left the kitchen after he'd gotten what he came for.

Caitlyn was surprised how Tiff changed her tone as soon as Elaine walked in. It was as if she was a different person. As if she were Jekyll and Hyde.

"Not to worry, you know where my room is. You can grab a blouse from my wardrobe."

"Thank you, Elaine."

What?

Tiff knew where Elaine's wardrobe was located? How many times had she been here?

The music continued to blare through the speakers and the sound of laughter filled the air. Caitlyn didn't know how many people were there, but it was a lot, quite a turnout for a child's party.

Later that afternoon, Caitlyn looked out the window and saw Riley playing with another cousin. She saw a few kids, but she didn't see Katie. She then went outside and looked around. Alarm rang in her mind. Fear gnawed through her. Where was her daughter?

Chapter 12 – The Past

She glanced at the baby in the car seat, alone. Where were her parents? It turned her stomach. Annoyance swept through her body at how careless parents could be. She'd spotted the mother and father of the child, presumably, having a drink. Their eyes weren't even on their baby. She knew what she had to do. She was going to teach them a lesson. She could care for their baby girl, more than they could. The girl had sweet rosy cheeks and wore a pink onesie with a pink blanket covering her. A cute little hat on her head. Sleeping. Without a care in the world. But she was going to take care of that child. She deserved to be the child's mother, not that woman having a drink and leaving her child in a crowded restaurant.

Her eyes gave a quick sweep of the area. There were no cameras in that area. None. Good. She would make her move. She was going to do what she thought was best for the child. She was going to adopt the child and protect her from careless people who didn't even care about her well-being. If she got away with it, if she was able to scoop the baby up in this noisy place and the parents didn't notice, well that was on them.

Always watch your baby.

Nervously, her hands trembled as she walked up to the car seat on the table with the lovely baby inside it.

She glanced over her shoulders. Would anyone notice? Was she being watched? She didn't think so.

Fear twisted her gut. What if she got caught? What would she say? You just don't walk into a restaurant and pick up a baby in a car seat. Embarrassment swirled through her of what would happen to her. It would be splashed all over the news. It would trend on social media and she could be vilified.

But her compulsion to take the child from what she perceived were uncaring parents was so strong. She had to do it. She had to do something.

As the restaurant and bar broke out into a song, it was evident the parents were probably drunk and busy singing. Why did they bring a baby there to that place? It looked as if it was some sort of party or celebration. One of theirs perhaps.

Well, she had to do it. She was already inches from the car seat. She had to do it. She was going to do it. She'd stolen things before but not a person. Could you steal a person? The pit of her stomach fell. None of the child's parents even turned around to check on their baby. What crazy fools. How could they abandon their baby in such a public place?

When she glanced over at the mother of the child, she noticed the woman had her handbag in front of her clutched in her hands. So, the handbag and its contents were more important to that woman than her own child.

She scoffed.

She held the handle and made a quick move and walked away, her steps swift and deliberate as if she knew what she was doing.

No one called out after her. No one noticed.

She glanced at the sweet little baby sleeping without a care in the world, without knowing what was happening. Without realizing that her own parents had let her down by ignoring her in a busy place. Her stomach fell as she realized that the child's mother didn't even realize she was gone. When would she know? Ten minutes later? An hour later? Either way, she would be long gone by then. She covered her head with the hood of her raincoat. It was beginning to drizzle but that wasn't the reason. She didn't want to be seen on cameras in the area just in case people had cameras on the cars or outside stores in the neighborhood.

She felt sick in her stomach doing this, but she felt the compulsion to do so. She had a problem. She took things. Things that didn't belong to her, but she was going to get help for it. She was going to do the therapy as the judge had suggested long ago. This would be the last thing she would steal.

But she knew deep down that she was no longer a thief. That sickened her to her stomach. She was no longer just a thief. She was...a kidnapper.

And it was time she left town and changed her identity. She would be someone else now. And her baby would be called by another name. She would choose a name for her new daughter. She breathed a sigh of relief until...

She heard sirens in the distance.

Chapter 13 – The Present

Worry gnawed at Caitlyn as she searched around the garden. She approached Riley.

"Where is she, Riley?"

"Where's who?"

"Katie! She was with you. Where is she?" Caitlyn's heartbeat pounded hard in her chest and in her throat. Sweat trickled down her spine. Fury rose through her.

"I guess she went inside to look for you," Riley said.

Caitlyn rushed back inside, her blood boiling inside her.

Katie. She needed to find her daughter.

Just then a flashback slid through her mind and her breathing almost stopped.

Was this karma? Was this payback for what she'd done?

Never take your eyes of your daughter.

Always watch her.

No. It couldn't be. It just couldn't be.

She realized she was breathing laboriously now. Her husband caught her as she was just about to make her way upstairs.

"You okay?"

"No, Katie is missing."

He didn't seem to be worried at all. He had a drink in his hand and looked as if he'd had quite a few. His skin was flushed. "Relax, she's probably playing outside," he said, as music played in the background.

"She's missing!" she shouted out, and instantly regretted taking out her frustration on Sam. "She isn't outside and don't tell me to relax," she said, trying not to sound as if she were attacking him.

"Then she's got to be around here somewhere."

Her stomach knotted into twists as she breathed heavily, looking around the large house, her shoes tapping on the marble floor. "Katie! Katie!" she shouted out.

Someone took her. But it couldn't have been a stranger. It had to be one of them. Somebody at the house. Someone who knew the family. It had to be. No strangers were around.

"Wait a minute. What about the security cameras?" she asked, desperate.

"She'll probably turn up. It's a big place. You know kids love to play hide and seek," Elaine said, casually as she walked up to her.

What was with her? Katie was her granddaughter. Didn't she care?

A sick feeling slid through her belly. What if Katie *was* missing? What if Caitlyn had to call the police? What would she say? What if they asked to see Katie's birth certificate? Would they do that? Caitlyn could be in trouble. They would find out what she did. Caitlyn may never see her daughter again.

Chapter 14 – The Present

Anxiety and fear swirled through Caitlyn's body. Numbness filled her limbs.

She's gone.

Katie was gone.

She'd looked everywhere for her. There was no way she could be on the premises.

"All right. Not to worry," Elaine said, cheerfully, as if she didn't believe Katie was gone. "Let's just organize a little search party, shall we." Elaine placed her wine glass on the table, not even looking in Caitlyn's direction. They thought she was mad, didn't they? They thought she was crazy. Didn't they realize that Katie was only three years old? Anything could happen to her.

Why did she take her eyes off her child? She never did that. She was at her in-law's home. She thought she'd be safe around the family and friends.

When Caitlyn's glance fell on Sam, she could see his face creased with worry. Well at least now he was taking things seriously.

This wasn't like Katie. She wouldn't just run off. Or would she?

Images of baby Katie lying asleep in her car seat at a restaurant swept across her mind. Then the heat of horror slid through her veins. Her spine prickled with nerves.

She was going to lose it. She was going to lose it any minute now if she didn't find her baby girl.

"Katie! Katie!" Caitlyn called out as she made her way around the massive mansion, rushing through the hallways and opening every single door that she could see. "Katie!"

Nothing.

Others were also calling her. When she reached into the main foyer, she could see her mother-in-law whispering to a friend of hers. Why wasn't she busy looking for her granddaughter? Just then, a strange look appeared in Elaine's eyes when she met Caitlyn's eyes. Did she know something?

Stop it, Caitlyn. Everything is going to be all right.

Would it?

She tried to swallow the hard lump in her throat but it was no use. She could barely breathe right now. Her heart hammered hard in her chest. She wanted to believe her little girl was all right. She wanted to believe she was hiding in some playroom at the mansion. But she couldn't believe that. Her heart won't let her. Something happened to Katie. She just knew it.

Caitlyn ignored her mother-in-law and continued to search as other guests were looking as well.

Just then Riley appeared.

"Riley, when was the last time you saw Katie?"

Riley shrugged. "She went inside the house. She wanted to get something to drink."

"What? Why didn't you say this before? She must have been looking for the kitchen." Caitlyn's eyes darted around the massive layout of the mansion. Katie could be anywhere. But she was never good with staircases. She would take her time.

A wave of nausea swept across her. Caitlyn suddenly felt dizzy with confusion. The room was swirling.

Then...

Caitlyn collapsed.

Everything around her went dark.

Chapter 15 – The Present

Little Katie was unaware she had been taken away from her so-called parents. She happily played with the little doll that had been given to her.

The plan worked beautifully. Get her to the mansion. Make sure the security cameras were not in working order and ensure there was a massive crowd and music blaring through the speakers. Everybody was busy, playing and laughing. Too busy to look around to make sure their little girl was sound and safe.

Well, this person knew very well what Caitlyn had done. They knew full well she was responsible for a horrible crime and now she would pay for it.

They would never find her. This person would make sure of it.

They would never even suspect what really happened to little Katie.

They glanced at the child again, hoping the child wouldn't recognize them. She seemed oblivious to what was going on as she played and danced to the music playing.

They could have gone to the police all those years ago when she was first taken from them, but they couldn't. Their own past would be revealed and they couldn't risk that. Instead they hunted Caitlyn down and waited for the right moment, the right time.

Katie would be safe now. She was where she should have been all these years. She was finally home. Her real home.

Chapter 16 – The Present

Caitlyn's head pounded like a base drum, throbbing with every beat of her pulse.

She lay on a bed, her eyelids heavy. "Where am I?" she asked, dazed. Her throat tight and dry. "Katie," she whispered. "Where's Katie?" She drifted off.

"Ssh, it's all right," Sam said, as he stroked her forehead. He had propped himself up on the bed beside her.

"What?" Her voice cracked. She forced her eyelids of open.

"We've called the police, dear," she heard Elaine's voice say. "It looks as if she wandered off."

"What?" *No!* "Katie doesn't wander off." The words barely left Caitlyn's throat.

It was painful to talk all of a sudden. Had she passed out again? Was that what happened to her earlier? Her medication. She needed to take her medication.

"All kids wander, dear. That's why it's so important to keep an eye on them. She's probably just somewhere around the grounds here. I have my staff outside looking for her. Not to worry." Elaine's tone was casual, too casual for Caitlyn's liking. Why was she being so damn cool about this? Was this a joke? Were they all just playing some sick joke with Caitlyn's mind?

Caitlyn knew her mother-in-law didn't like her that much. Caitlyn knew Elaine didn't think much of her. She knew Elaine had preferred Sam's ex, Jessica. He'd told her many times and Elaine had told her too in so many words...Jessica this and Jessica that. But that was all in the past now. Caitlyn was the one who had married Sam, not his ex.

She wished she'd just woken up from a nightmare. She wished it had all been a horrible dream and her Katie was safe and with her now.

Oh, where was she? Where was her precious little girl? Where was her daughter?

Sweat trickled down Caitlyn's spine, the glands in her mouth dried up, fear splintered her heart.

No. No, this could not be happening. The police could not be involved. What if they discovered her past?

She'd lose Katie either way.

She could not allow this to happen. But then again, she wanted her baby back. She wanted her daughter to be safe. What if a stranger had taken her?

But it couldn't be. How could a stranger just walk into a private mansion and take a child without anyone knowing? It must have been an inside job. Somebody from the family's inner circle took Katie. But who? And why?

Fear twisted Caitlyn's gut as she struggled to prop herself up on the bed. "Why am I here? I need to look for our daughter."

"It's okay, babe, you just passed out. Probably didn't have much to eat earlier."

That was true. She'd been so busy today. She didn't have time to sit down and eat a meal. But that wasn't the reason she passed out. Caitlyn knew the real reason. Shock. Panic. Anxiety. Her blood pressure probably dropped or rose to a dangerous level and she passed out. Not enough oxygenated blood to her brain, that's probably what it was. It was the fear of losing the one thing she truly ever wanted in her life. A daughter. Her daughter. The daughter she'd rescued from those horrible parents.

Caitlyn crumbled inside. A weight settled in her heart. This was her worst nightmare, ever! Her daughter had gone missing. Right under her nose. She was never going to see her daughter again, was she?

No, she had to fight that horrible feeling. Caitlyn needed to be strong for her Katie. She was going to get her back. She was going to find out who took her and she was going to get revenge. Katie was her daughter. She loved her more than anything in the world. She would stop at nothing to get her back.

Chapter 17 – The Present

Moments later, a few police cars showed up. A strange appearance in an otherwise cozy upscale neighborhood. One didn't usually see police in this affluent neighborhood. Caitlyn pulled the curtain back as she stood in the guest room at her mother-in-law's mansion. She saw Elaine talking casually to a detective. Her mother-in-law threw her head back in laughter.

What?

Why would she do that?

For a woman who'd just lost her granddaughter, her behavior was strange and it unnerved Caitlyn even more.

Her granddaughter was missing! How could she be so callous about it all?

Then again, it didn't seem like any urgency, did it?

There was no proof that Katie was kidnapped or abducted. In their eyes, she had probably just wandered off. But she knew her little girl. Katie would never just wander off.

Guilt swirled through her body.

She fought back tears.

No.

This couldn't be happening.

She needed her little girl back. She wanted Katie back, safe and sound.

Oh, where was her daughter?

Sam was already outside looking for her daughter on the grounds, his cell phone pressed to his ears. He was probably talking to a friend asking for more help. She wanted to join the search party. Her limbs felt numb, but she didn't care. She slowly made her way towards the door when she heard footsteps along the corridor outside her door.

Her heart leaped in her chest. Was it Katie?

She whipped open the door and her face fell.

"Tiff," she said.

"Hey, you. How are you holding up? I heard Katie was missing and I came right back."

Caitlyn swallowed hard, her heartbeat still thrashing inside her chest. "Yes, she's not here. I don't know where she is." She started to break down, tears flooding down her face. She was falling apart now. She'd held up as much as she could to be strong and sound so that she could find Katie but seeing Tiff there, her best friend, she finally had the courage to just let it all out.

"It's okay," Tiff said hugging her. "It's going to be all right. She's got to be around here somewhere. She couldn't have gotten far."

"How did you hear?"

A shadow of guilt spread across Tiff's face. "Sam called me and told me."

"Oh," Caitlyn said.

There was an awkward pause between them. Was that who Sam was on the phone with? Tiffany?

She then grabbed tissues from the tissue box on the table and dabbed her eyes. She breathed in a deep sigh. Right now, she didn't have the energy to try and process what Tiffany had just told her. Why would her husband call Caitlyn's best friend?

Still, Tiff was Katie's godmother. But at the moment, Caitlyn only had enough energy to find her daughter. She felt a wave of guilt over hating Tiff for a brief second when she told her that Sam had called her to tell her Katie was missing. After all, Tiff was there to help, wasn't she?

"Thanks for coming," she said. "I'm going to go out there and help."

"Shouldn't you take it easy?" Tiff asked, her voice soothing.

"No!" Caitlyn said, and instantly regretted sounding sharp. "I'm sorry, I'm just all over the place. The police are here too and they're probably going to want to get some information from me."

"I think Sam already gave them a photo of Katie," Tiff said.

Again, shock slid down Caitlyn's spine. How did Tiff know that? They were probably wondering why the child's mother wasn't down there with them.

"I'm going downstairs now," Caitlyn said, her lips pinched into a thin line.

She was going to help find her daughter. And yes, she would face the police if she had to. She knew it was inevitable that she would have to speak with them.

They couldn't possibly know who she really was. And even if they suspected something about Caitlyn's past, she already had a scripted response ready.

Chapter 18– The Present

Moments later, Caitlyn found herself in the grand study of the mansion along with officers of the law, her mother-in-law, Sam and Tiffany. She wondered why Tiffany had come into the meeting. This was a family matter, even though Tiffany was the godmother. She didn't feel comfortable with her being there right now.

What if the cops asked Caitlyn questions that she couldn't answer? What would happen then? Would her secret be revealed?

Her stomach contorted into knots; her palms moistened under the tension. One of the detectives came over to where she stood.

"Mrs...."

"Caitlyn. Please just call me Caitlyn."

"Caitlyn. I'm Detective Smith and this is my associate, Detective Palmer."

Caitlyn nodded, solemnly.

"I'm sorry about what happened. We're going to try to find your daughter." Detective Smith glanced at both Caitlyn and Sam. "Now, I understand that your daughter has wandered off..."

"Yes," Sam said.

"I...I don't think so. I think she may have been abducted," Caitlyn said, contradicting Sam. They'd both spoken at the same time. Caitlyn bit down on her lower lip. Should she have just said her daughter was missing? What if they probed further into why Caitlyn believed Katie was abducted? Oh, why didn't she keep her mouth shut?

She noticed when the detective gave his partner a strange look. She continued on with her questions, holding her pen in her hand and her notebook poised to write down more notes. She wondered why they didn't just record everything, but she supposed it was safer to gather all information on a tangible item just in case the recording failed or glitched.

Caitlyn swallowed hard, hoping they wouldn't notice how guilty she looked. She knew cops had a sixth sense when it came to spotting a liar. But she wasn't a liar.

Katie was missing.

She's missing.

And that's all there was to it.

The only trouble was, would they believe Katie was her daughter?

Don't look guilty, Caitlyn. Be calm. Be calm. Suck in a deep breath. Nice and easy. In one, two, three. Out, one, two, three...

"Ma'am," Detective Smith said, as Detective Palmer looked directly into Caitlyn's eyes as if trying to read her or study her or try to place where he may have seen her before. She broke his gaze and focused her attention on Detective Smith.

"Do you have a copy of Katie's birth certificate?" Smith asked her.

Caitlyn's core body temperature dropped. Her chest tightened with panic. Fear hit her like icy water.

"Why does that matter right now?" Sam asked, anger flashing in his eyes. "My daughter is missing. A birth certificate is not going to find her now. It doesn't have a GPS locator on it."

"It's okay," Caitlyn said, trying to remain calm to pacify the situation, her heart still thumped hard in her chest, so hard she was sure they could hear her rapid heartbeat.

Sam had a temper and yes, she agreed with him that they should just put all their focus and energy on finding Katie. Did they seriously think the whole family was making up a child that didn't really exist in real life? Didn't Sam show them pictures of Katie on his phone? He had as much as she did. Thousands of images on the phone of happy times and happy moments.

Except...

Images of when Katie was born.

"You believe your daughter was abducted, Ma'am?" Detective Smith asked.

"I don't know. She's...she's just missing. She doesn't usually wander off like that. She's not a wanderer."

Now Caitlyn was beginning to regret telling them she thought her daughter was kidnapped. She had no proof. Just an inkling. A sick feeling in the pit of her stomach.

Then a gnawing thought clawed away at her.

She remembered that there was a database of missing children in the state. Thousands of children go missing every year and many are found safe and sound early. But for those who were missing for an extended period of time, even years, their information was stored in a database until they were found.

Birth certificates were flagged, so the registrar of births and deaths would be notified by law enforcement agencies.

Oh, what had Caitlyn gotten herself into?

There was no good possible way out of this—not for her at least. Or Sam. What would his family think if they knew the horrible truth?

Everything in her new life in Sweetness County had seem so picture perfect up to this point. They had everything Caitlyn had ever dreamed of growing up. A loving close-knit family, a safe and friendly community, middle-class suburban life, friends, family, a nice green front yard for her child to play in and, of course, a lovely home with a white-picket fence. She made sure to have one installed at the front of their front lawn just as she'd seen on Instagram.

"Her birth certificate is at home, of course. We don't carry it around with us," she said, trying to sound as sweet and cooperative and polite as she could.

"Of course not," Detective Smith said, "We'll have some officers visit your home soon."

Caitlyn's stomach tightened into knots. Of course they would.

"We are going to look at every possible angle, Ma'am," Detective Smith assured.

The detective then gazed into Caitlyn's eyes as if trying to create a profile on her. What had Elaine said to the cops earlier when she was outside talking to them and holding her head back in laughter? Now paranoia washed over Caitlyn in waves of nausea.

Did they all think she was crazy? Did they think Katie was just out there hiding amongst the trees. It looked like a bloody forest out there on the land. It didn't even look like private property. But then again her in-laws were wealthy. Very wealthy. And very well connected.

Caitlyn paced by the stone fireplace back and forth while holding her arms rubbing them as if a chill overcame her. She felt the chill of the past come back to haunt her. There was just no way in hell she could be calm right now. But what surprised her was how calm everybody else in the room were. Did the cops suspect her of doing something wrong? Did they know her secret? Was her past coming back to destroy her and all that she cared about.

Katie.

All she wanted was her daughter back. Her beloved little girl. The girl she cared for since she was a newborn. She wanted her back. Every fiber in her body ached to hold little Katie again in her arms and to tell her that everything was going to be okay, that her horrible parents could never abandon her again. Ever. She'd vowed to take care of her and she'd let her down.

Katie was missing.

What was she doing right now?

Caitlyn glared out the window noticing the overcast sky. It was getting dark. Her little girl was out there somewhere. Was she alone? Was she hurt? What if she fell and hurt herself? Was she crying for her mommy? The more the thoughts swirled in Caitlyn's mind, the crazier she felt. She trembled with fury. She couldn't stay put. She *had* to do something.

Chapter 19 – The Past

"What compels you to steal, Mary?" the counselor asked her, pointedly. He was growing impatient with her now and she knew it. A vein throbbed in his temple. His brows furrowed as he directed his gaze on her.

She sat there dazed, not wanting to open up to him or to anyone for that matter.

"Mary, the sooner we discuss this, the better for you."

Again, silence on her part.

Was he hoping she would incriminate herself? She sat in his office, staring out the window, her eyes capturing the crisp orange and yellow leaves of the trees outside. It looked more like an orange forest of trees. Fall was her favorite season. She didn't know why; there was just something warm and cozy about the season. A time for sitting by the fireplace, donning cozy sweaters, pumpkin spice lattes and watching her favorite shows on TV, getting crazy discounts and mega deals on Black Friday shopping sales. She loved the countdowns and cyber shopping sales too. At least then she didn't have to go out into a crowd of people to fight for the last sale item on the department store shelf.

Everything seemed so laxed during holiday seasons too. Many celebrated Thanksgiving with their families. That was the only thing that troubled her. Her family. They were not what one would call warm and cozy. They were about image. Image was everything to her parents and they made it known every single day how much she threatened that image. The one they portrayed to the public, to their friends and colleagues and followers on social media.

She was an embarrassment to them, wasn't she?

They didn't tell her outright, but she knew it. She felt it deep down to her core. And she loathed their actions for making her feel that way.

He grew more impatient, sighing deeply. His sigh was so deep, she was sure that people in the parking lot outside could hear him.

He scribbled some notes on a sheet of paper attached to his clipboard. She could only guess what he was putting down on the page. She couldn't care less right now, but deep down she knew that was the wrong attitude to have. She should care. She should care what he said, because it would be his testimony that could set her free.

She swallowed hard, vowing this time to cooperate as best as she could.

"I don't steal," she finally said, her voice soft as a whisper and hoarse from dryness. She hadn't had anything to eat or drink all morning. She was mini fasting. No particular reason. She just didn't want anything to drink.

"Can I get you a glass of water or something to eat?" he asked, as if he could read her mind. He was probably given a report about her and told she had refused to eat anything the staff had given her at the facility.

"No, I'm fine, thank you."

"You don't sound fine," he said.

"I should know how I feel."

He continued. "Okay, yes, you should know how you feel, but I'm here to help you, Mary. We all want to see you get better."

"Do you?"

"What do you mean by that?"

"My parents hired you, didn't they? They stuck me in here. They want to see me get better or they want to see me disappear?"

"Mary, your parents love you. They are concerned about you."

"They are concerned about their image. They're not very nice people." Why was she saying that about them? Maybe not getting enough nutrients to her brain was affecting her thinking. In fact, she knew it was. She should really take him up on his offer to have something to eat and drink now.

But what if they spiked her food or drink? She didn't trust him. She didn't trust her parents. She didn't trust anyone.

"Mary, why do you say that?"

"They don't understand me. I don't steal and they know it. I only rescue."

"You rescue."

"Yes, I rescue those who have been abandoned, whether a puppy or..."

"Or a baby?" he probed, finishing her sentence; his pen hovered over his page. He wanted her to admit stealing a baby.

Well that was something she was never going to admit.

She burned with humiliation. She wasn't going to do that. She wanted to disappear. She knew she shouldn't steal; it was a terrible compulsion. There was no excuse for it. She needed help. She needed a way out. Guilt and shame flooded over her.

"Mary," he said, his voice softer. "Are you doing this to get your parents' attention? Is that what this is all about?"

Now, it was her turn to be stunned. She glanced up at him, her jaw wide open in shock. "Is that what they've been telling you? That I want to get their *attention*?"

Indignation filled her yet deep down she knew she had no right to feel indignant. What she'd done was wrong. It was terrible. It was an awful thing to do. Yet she'd done it. Why?

She racked her brain over and over again trying to dig deep and find out where she'd gone wrong. What was the real reason?

Well, it certainly wasn't to get her parents' attention. She already knew she was not on their list of priorities.

She never did fit into their world. Into their neat little inner circle. Their perfect image of perfect people. She was not perfect. Far from it. But she was lost. And she wanted desperately to find a way out. All the other things she'd stolen was inexcusable

Yet in her mind, she did it for the right reasons.

Were they planning to lock her away—forever?

What were they going to do to her now?

Chapter 20 – The Present

"Can you tell us what your daughter was wearing when you last saw her?" Detective Smith asked, distracting Caitlyn's thoughts.

She'd been staring out the tall glass French doors of the study, looking out at the massive gardens as police and visitors combed the area, looking for Katie. Her precious little girl. She should be out there with them, looking, calling out Katie's name, hoping she'd run out from hiding behind one of the tall trees. She didn't want to be stuck in here in a room filled with officers and her in-laws.

Caitlyn sucked in a deep breath, trying hard to calm her nerves, though it was no use. She could feel her throat tighten, her mouth dry up, her pulse quickening with anxiety.

The question then whirled around in her mind. What was she wearing when she last saw her?

Annoyance flared inside her. Why were they asking her this now? What were they asking her mother-in-law and husband earlier? Didn't they already *have* that information? Or maybe they wanted to see if everyone's story collaborated.

"You can't miss her, she was wearing her bright yellow raincoat," Caitlyn said, her stomach sinking.

The irony of the situation was not lost on her. Her daughter Katie had been wearing a bright yellow raincoat when she played outside with her cousins yet no one noticed her missing.

She wanted to heave at the thought. Why wasn't she outside with the kids? She thought they'd had supervision outside. They were on private property. How did her own child go missing? What happened?

Did she scream out when she was being kidnapped? She felt the officers were thinking the same thing. If she were being snatched up by a total stranger, surely she would have made a sound. Surely someone must have spotted a stranger outside with the kids.

That's assuming it *was* a stranger who'd abducted her little girl.

The detective scribbled down some words on her note pad.

"Was your daughter upset when you last saw her?"

"No. She was happy," Caitlyn said, biting down on her lower lip. Every muscle in her body tensed up.

"Look, she's got to be here somewhere," Sam chimed in, pacing by the fireplace. "She couldn't have gotten far." He ran his fingers through his dark brown hair. This was the first time she'd seen him getting tense since Katie disappeared. It was probably finally striking him that this was serious. That she was really missing. That someone could have taken her.

The thought was unthinkable, but they had to do something.

The detective looked up at Sam. "Yes, sir. We're doing everything in our power to find her safely."

Caitlyn also paced and rubbed her arms as she hugged herself, wishing she could be hugging her daughter now.

"Can't you just put out an Amber alert?"

Earlier, Caitlyn would be terrified of that suggestion. She knew that there was a risk of everything crumbling around her.

There was a risk of Caitlyn being exposed and possibly arrested. But there was something that overrode that feeling.

Love.

Motherly love.

The fierce, protective, altruistic love a mother had for her child. That's all that mattered right now. That was her dominant feeling. Fear of losing her daughter. The burning urge to protect her daughter.

In her mind, she was Katie's mother.

She loved Katie more than anything in this world. And right now, she didn't care if her life came crumbling down around her. The fear of public humiliation, if it ever came to light what she'd done, didn't even seem to matter now. It all paled compared to Katie's safety. She just wanted to make sure her daughter was safe from harm. She wanted to make sure she was all right.

"We need to have a few things in place first, Ma'am."

"A few things? Like what? My daughter is *missing*!"

"Yes, Ma'am but in this town, we need to make sure the child was abducted and hasn't just wandered away. We would also need a description of a vehicle and a description of the abductor. We have neither right now. We have people outside right now as we speak, combing the area."

She knew she should feel a sense of relief they were hard on the case but she didn't. Far from it. She wanted Katie back now. She wanted her daughter back.

"Oh, that's just great, isn't it?" Sam's sarcasm laced his tone. Caitlyn felt the same way. They should just do everything in their power and stop worrying about little red tape.

Their daughter was missing!

"The fact is, she is or was on family property. We need to check everywhere first."

Elaine's cheeks flushed.

Caitlyn narrowed her eyes in suspicion as she glanced over at her mother-in-law.

Her skin prickled. She suppressed a shudder. What was her mother-in-law hiding?

"You mean you're going to search my house?" Elaine asked, nervously fidgeting with the pearls around her neck. Her tone had an air of incredulous to it. She should be eager for the cops to help find her granddaughter.

"Yes, Ma'am, if it's all right with you," the detective said, her tone firm. It was more of a statement than permission. It was as if the detective challenged her.

This was a different officer than the one Caitlyn had seen talking and laughing with Elaine earlier outside.

Caitlyn could just imagine her mother-in-law reporting this officer later.

"But we've already searched inside here," Elaine continued. "She's clearly not in here."

Indignation rolled through Caitlyn. *Seriously?* Katie was missing and all her mother-in-law could think about was the cops searching her home?

What about Katie's safety? As each moment and minute ticked by, it was riskier for her little girl to be out there alone.

Caitlyn's stomach churned thinking about her little three-year-old out there somewhere, missing.

What if Katie *was* in fact hiding somewhere? Or worse. What if someone was hiding Katie inside this grand mansion? Was her daughter terrified? Hurt?

Caitlyn would lose her mind; she would die if anything ever happened to her daughter.

Right now Caitlyn trusted no one. Because in her books, someone close to her took her daughter away. Someone in the family circle. The more she thought about it, the more she knew that it couldn't be just a random stranger walking on the premises of the Reede Mansion and grabbing a child that was a total stranger to them.

According to statistics, more kids were abducted by someone they knew than a total stranger. Less than one per cent of kids were abducted by strangers, Caitlyn remembered reading somewhere.

"Yes," Elaine finally said, waving her hand dismissively. Her lips pinched into a thin line.

Something seemed off right now. This was so untypical in Elaine's behavior. Why was she acting so callously about this? Was she hiding something?

The detective then motioned for some officers to start searching the mansion.

Again, Caitlyn paced nervously. It could take forever in a house, if one could call it a house, of that size. How long would they take? She could be anywhere by now.

"Are there any security cameras around?" the detective then asked. "We would like to take a look at the footage to see if we see her there and where she's gone."

"Of course," Caitlyn said, anxiously looking around. There were cameras everywhere at the Reede's mansion. Those hidden little dark round glass things followed you around everywhere you went in the home and around the property. Her heart palpitated in her chest. Why didn't she think of that before?

That's what happened when your mind was stressed out, you forgot things. You forget the obvious.

Elaine cleared her throat. "Yes, well, my husband and I worry about privacy, so..." Elaine's cheeks flushed. "Well, the cameras are not really...you see..."

"They're dummy cameras?" the detective finished for her, incredulously.

"Well, I wouldn't call them that. They're just not turned on, you understand? We are very private here. We don't really trust this whole Wi-Fi thing and...you know..." Elaine hesitated. She almost never hesitated. This was so uncharacteristic of her.

"What?" Caitlyn said, astonished. She turned to Sam and he seemed equally surprised.

All this time, she thought the house was properly secured with security cameras and they were fakes? Fakes? Much like her in-laws, she thought bitterly, wanting to lash out at anyone. How could they? Those cameras were her last hope of finding her daughter or at least finding out what happened to Katie, where she disappeared to.

Oh, this was not good. This was the last thing she needed. Caitlyn was counting on those cameras revealing what happened to Katie. Shit! Now they would never know. She assumed her rich in-laws had working cameras.

It was all a façade. The last thing she needed right now. Was everything a façade with the Reedes?

"Right," the detective said, scribbling something on her notepad. "Do you mind if we still take a look?" she asked.

Elaine looked uneasy at first, then she gave a fake smile that didn't touch her eyes. "Sure, why not?" she finally said, her tone betraying her facial expression.

Inside, Caitlyn was deeply relieved the cops didn't just take Elaine's word for it that her cameras were not working. But there was a sinking feeling in the pit of Caitlyn's stomach that the cops were not going to find anything on those security cameras. The cameras were probably not recording.

She'd read somewhere that people who were not comfortable being recorded over Wi-Fi often had dummy cameras to deter criminals. But Caitlyn didn't believe in that. If someone was breaking the law or breaking into your home you would want to catch them and have them brought to justice. What was the point in having cameras that didn't work?

"Cameras not on," another officer said later.

Caitlyn's knees felt numb and weak. She felt as if she were going to faint.

Now what were they going to do?

They were in the dark now.

Shit. Caitlyn cursed under her breath. Each passing moment, the risks of never finding her daughter again increased.

The darker it grew outside, the more worry swept over Caitlyn like a dark cloud of despair.

Where was Katie right now?

Would Caitlyn ever get her daughter back?

Chapter 21 – The Present

"We'll need a list of everyone who was here at the party today," Detective Smith said, after officers combed through the mansion. "And no one leave, please." Her tone was direct and authoritative.

As everyone stood in the grand study like a party of suspects while officers searched outside, everyone was questioned.

Caitlyn looked around, eyeing everyone with suspicion. It could be anyone of them that saw Katie last. What if they were responsible? She looked at the butler. He was a short stocky man with a thick moustache. She'd seen Katie talking to him earlier when he went outside to deliver a tray full of ice-cream cones. She didn't know why he served that on a cool day like today. But she guessed the kids all loved ice cream in any season.

Her eyes then drew to Gerard, the gardener. He was outside tending to the leaves while watching the kids too. She never liked the way he kept eyeing Katie and her cousins. She was about to go outside and say something but she got distracted.

Did *he* have something to do with Katie going missing?

Caitlyn's heart pumped hard and fast in her chest just thinking about that.

She watched as he looked downward while the officers questioned him. Why wouldn't he look them in the eyes? Did he have something to hide?

What about Lynn, the housekeeper or the other cleaning staff? Or what about Deanna, Elaine's personal assistant who worked at the home office? Caitlyn had only seen Deanna a hand full of times, but she was always quiet whenever Caitlyn and Katie came by the house to visit the Reedes. Too quiet for Caitlyn's liking. What if Deanna had something to do with it.

It had to be someone who was there today at the party. Someone close to the family. Someone who was trusted.

No, that's crazy. Caitlyn squeezed her eyes shut and drew in a deep breath. She knew she had to get control of herself before she drove herself crazy. Then how would she be able to find her daughter? She needed to keep her mind together. She would be no use to Katie if she went completely insane. There were too many thoughts, millions of thoughts, and emotions rushing through her mind and her soul right now.

She could feel herself hyperventilating, as she hugged her arms across her chest defensively while eyeing everyone as if watching them would make them want to confess. But confess to what? That they knew nothing?

They weren't Katie's parents; she and Sam were. And they'd let their daughter down. They would never forgive themselves if anything happened to their little girl.

Deep breath, Caitlyn. Take a nice deep breath.

"How long has Gerard been working here?" Caitlyn whispered quietly to Sam while they stood by themselves in another corner of the now filled study.

Sam shrugged. "Don't know."

"You don't know? Where did your mother find him? What happened to what's his name?"

"Who Travis? He retired."

"How long ago was that? I thought he was off sick or something?"

"Yes...no....look, I don't remember." Sam ran his fingers through his hair. "Why are you asking me this now?" His tone was louder.

"I'm just saying, why did Travis leave?"

"Listen, ask my mom, okay. I think someone died in his family and he left to take care of their house or something."

"So she hired Gerard? Where did she find him?"

"I think he's related to Travis. Travis recommended him."

Caitlyn's skin prickled. She didn't know why but she just thought it was all suspicious. Travis wasn't that old to begin with. She was surprised he even retired. Did he come into some money? Something didn't add up. She just didn't buy it. Any of it.

She swallowed hard. Her eyes cast on Gerard again. As if he sensed he was being watched from across the room, he looked up and directly into Caitlyn's eyes. She shivered inside at his dark gaze.

He then looked away.

What was that about?

She had a strange feeling about him. A very strange feeling.

"The cops should search his house."

"What? Are you crazy? Gerard's been here this whole time."

"Has he?"

"Caitlyn, I want to find Katie as much as you do but we can't go searching everybody's houses."

"And why not? Our daughter is missing and someone here knows what happened!" Her tone was louder than she'd wanted. All heads turned around. She sucked in a deep breath, trying to calm herself.

"It's going to be all right," Sam said, holding her again.

The chatter in the room had quieted for a moment, but then all eyes were on her with sorrow. She noticed they all felt sorry for her. She didn't need or want their sympathy; she wanted their answers. The truth.

Right now, she didn't care if they thought she was a hysterical mother. She was a mother who wanted her daughter back now.

Later, Gerard left the study after the cops finished with him.

Why weren't they going to visit his home?

She immediately rushed to the window to see where he was going. Was he going back outside to the garden? Or was he going home?

She followed his moves and he looked around outside and then reached into his pocket to pull something out. Was it a cell phone? No, it was a cigarette pack. He then put it back in his pocket and looked around nervously.

Then...

She saw Tiffany walking over to him.

They both looked around and started talking.

What the hell was going on?

Why on earth was Tiffany, her best friend, speaking to the gardener? Did she know him personally?

"Honey," Sam interrupted her from behind. "What are you doing? Come let's go."

"Why is Tiff talking to Gerard?"

"Oh, God, Caitlyn, just let it go. She can talk to whomever she wants. They had nothing to do with it. Katie probably just ran off. We'll find her."

He was changing his tune. Did he believe all that crap they each said, that Katie had a fight with one of her little cousins. Because that seemed to be what the other kids had told the cops. She didn't believe it for one minute.

"I don't think Katie ran off because of a fight."

"Listen, you heard what Riley and others said. She wanted to play on the bike and she had a fight with her cousin. Kids fight over toys all the time."

"Not Katie."

He sighed deeply. "Honey, I think it is a possibility that she just got upset and ran off to hide somewhere. We have to look at that option too."

She glanced into his eyes incredulously. Did he really believe that? Did he really believe that his little girl ran off and hid because of some fight with a toddler or one of her cousins? That didn't seem like Katie.

She was taken. Someone took her away.

And Caitlyn wasn't going to stop until she found her daughter safe and sound.

Before Caitlyn knew it, the evening flew by. Everyone at the party was questioned by the police officers and detectives on the scene. That included Riley, her cousin, who had last seen her; Katie's other cousins;

Tiffany, Caitlyn's best friend; Lynn, the housekeeper; Alex, the chef; Lou, the butler, the other cleaning staff; and Gerard, the gardener.

Everybody was questioned.

The police then told them to keep in touch if they remembered anything.

In Caitlyn's eyes that just wasn't enough.

Why didn't the cops go to each of the guests' and staff members' homes?

That would satisfy her that every nook and cranny was being checked.

What if one of them gained Katie's trust and kidnapped her and brought her to their home and then returned to the party as if nothing happened?

That would make more sense. She didn't scream out or alert anyone that she was being kidnapped because they were already at the home mingling with guests. Katie trusted her kidnapper.

Caitlyn's stomach lurched at the thought. She felt as if she was going to heave any moment now.

Chapter 22 – The Present

"I'm so sorry," Elaine had said later as Caitlyn and Sam were leaving with the police to go to their own home.

"It's not your fault, Mom," Sam said, his voice hoarse with pain. Anger flashed in his eyes as he spoke.

Caitlyn could tell he was torn. He loved his mother but he loved his daughter and at the end of the day, his daughter had gone missing from his mother's supposedly secure mansion. The home where his daughter should have been safe at a party for one of her cousins.

Whether or not he was thinking those thoughts, it certainly crossed Caitlyn's mind.

She was too numb to speak right now. She didn't want to leave the premise. Katie could be there somewhere, hiding...or hidden.

Tired and frustrated they drove back with the police to their home on the west side. It seemed so empty, so cold, so desperate as they pulled up to the curb.

Katie wasn't there.

Tears welled up in her eyes thinking of her precious little girl. Where was she?

As she got out of the car, she noticed the neighbor Steve and his wife Mary across the street. They were out on their front lawn talking with a neighbor. Was everybody aware now of Katie's disappearance?

Her heart hammered in her chest. She hoped so. She hoped they would all be on the lookout.

Just then Steve looked up and saw her. He then turned his head away.

What?

"What are you doing?" Sam said as he noticed she stood outside her home looking across the street.

"It's the new neighbors. Steve and Mary."

"And?"

She shook her head confused. "I need to speak to them."

She walked over to the house before anyone could stop her. Sam followed close behind. The officers looked on from where they had stood outside her house. They were ready to follow them inside but anger flared inside Caitlyn.

"Hi," she said. "We met the other day."

"Yes," Steve said. "I'm sorry your daughter is missing," he said, stuttering.

That's strange. How did he know she was missing? Shouldn't he have asked 'have you found your daughter yet?'

"We're still looking for her," she said. She then turned to Mary. "Hi, you must be Mary."

The woman said nothing at first. She just looked down to the ground. How odd. Did she not have a voice?

"I'm sorry, my wife is not well," Steve said. "Go back inside, darling," he said, stuttering.

The woman then left without saying a word. What an odd pair.

"Please let us know if you hear anything," Sam said, frustration in his voice. "I'm Sam, by the way."

"Oh, yes, you're Katie's dad."

"How did you know my daughter's name?" Caitlyn asked, suspiciously.

"That's what the neighbors have been saying," he said.

"Come on, babe," Sam said, wearily. "Cops are waiting for us."

Caitlyn hesitated for a moment and then sighed deeply, feeling despair whirl through her body.

She then turned around after saying goodbye and walked across the street, overcast evening skies above. The branches of the trees swayed in the wind along with her patience.

"What was that about?" Sam whispered as they walked back to the house.

She stopped for a moment so that no one would hear them.

"I stole his watch the other day."

"What? Jeez, Caitlyn, why the hell did you do that for?"

"I'm so sorry."

"So you think because you stole his watch, he stole Katie? Is that it? Is that the reason you just ran over there?"

"I walked over there, I didn't run. And yes, I...I don't know why I did it, but I returned it. I wasn't going to even tell you but now, I'm worried. I'm worried about Katie and..." Her thoughts were all over the place right now. A whirlwind of doubt swirled over her. She didn't know what to think. She just didn't trust anybody. She suspected everyone.

Was it the creepy neighbors? Was it Elaine? Was it Tiffany who so badly wanted a child. Tiff's ex had left her because she couldn't give him one. Tiff had told her that she couldn't have children yet she had stretch marks all over her belly indicating that she had been pregnant. Caitlyn was lost. A sob escaped her lips. Her nerves were rattled. She was breaking down. She had to be strong for her little girl but she didn't feel strong right now.

He hugged her and for the first time since Katie went missing, she felt his support. She felt comforted given the circumstances. Sam didn't hate her. She didn't know what she would do if he turned against her...

He never did ask to see Katie's birth certificate when they had gotten married. He trusted her. And why wouldn't he? She'd trusted him with her life. Most newlyweds don't ask to see every single piece of ID their new spouse had but maybe they should.

Later, the detectives spoke with Sam and Caitlyn for some time, asking more questions, asking to see photos and Katie's room. Her heart swelled just thinking of how much Katie enjoyed the way Caitlyn decorated her little room like a princess. Her favorite colors and Disney characters on the wall and in her toybox. She loved her little room. Would she be crying to be home right now? To be with her family that loved her? To be in her own room with all her toys?

When they asked to see her birth certificate, Caitlyn carefully looked in the safe box but it was missing.

"Oh, that's right," she said. "I meant to replace it. I'd lost it."

"You did?" Sam said.

"Yes, darling. I forgot to tell you. I didn't think I'd need it for now. I had already applied for a replacement." She swallowed hard.

The cops were probably not going to buy it. They were too smart for that. Or would they? Would they overlook the fact that she was a grief-stricken mother who'd just lost her daughter—sort of?

She dared not meet their gaze. She wasn't good at lying to authorities. They could always tell she was lying if she tried to look them in the eyes.

Detective Smith sighed heavily.

"We'll request a copy, if you like, given the circumstances...."

"It might be in the mailbox. I'll have to check."

The mailbox was quite a distance from the home. It was a community mailbox since it was a new subdivision in the area."

"Very well then...we'll just ask you a few questions."

The detective asked for Katie's date of birth and other information.

It was only a matter of time now. They would find out the truth.

Chapter 23 – The Present

"Here's my card," Detective Smith said as she handed her business card to Caitlyn. "Please let us know if you find anything new or if someone tries to contact you."

She sighed a deep relief that they were finally going to look at the angle that possibly Katie was kidnapped. There was no way she could have just wandered off like that. Not her little Katie.

"We will," Sam said as he hugged Caitlyn.

After the officers left, Caitlyn knew they could return any moment with news that she could be taken into custody. It was nighttime now. But in the morning, once the registrar opened up, Caitlyn could be arrested.

She couldn't rest knowing that.

Just then she glanced out the window. She thought she caught a shadow of a person standing across the street and she gasped.

Chapter 24 – The Present

"Are you all right?" Sam asked, coming over to Caitlyn as she stood at the window looking out.

"There, across the street. There's a woman. Is it...is it Mary?"

"Mary?"

"Steve's wife."

He looked. "I don't know. Want me to go out there?" he asked, getting ready to leave.

"No."

The woman then looked away and walked off.

Maybe it wasn't Steve's wife Mary. Maybe it was someone else.

Caitlyn swallowed hard.

"Do you think we should tell the police?"

"Tell them what? There was a woman on the sidewalk across the street? I don't think that's breaking the law."

"Yes, but...what if..."

"What if what?" Annoyance swept into his tone. She could tell what it was. He needed a drink, badly. But she didn't want him to get crazy drunk. She needed him sober. With her. Helping her to figure out how to find their daughter. She needed his emotional support. Whenever he drank, he was no good to anyone. Especially not to himself.

"Never mind," she said, feeling defeated.

Later that evening, neither Sam nor Caitlyn could sleep. They wracked their brains trying to figure out what happened.

Sam said he was going back out to search around, drive around and see if he found her, but Caitlyn begged him not to go alone.

He insisted on going alone. She wanted to come with him. There was no way she could just sit there when her daughter was out there.

Caitlyn's phone started to ping like crazy as messages and texts flooded through. She knew that some of the guests had already posted on social media. And she could just imagine what her clients were saying.

But right now, her focus was on Katie. She didn't have time to scroll through all of her messages.

Unless...

She whipped her phone out of her purse and frantically scanned her messages, hoping, praying there would be some contact from the kidnapper. She was sure Katie was taken. And she had an idea by whom.

Chapter 25 – The Past

Mary had to get away.

Nervously, she briefly glanced back, looking up at the building where they'd been keeping her. She pulled her hood over her head; glad she wore a hooded jacket today. It was freezing outside. Her wavy hair peeked through the sides of her hood.

Would security notice her?

By the time they found out she'd knocked the counselor out then closed the door behind her, leaving him alone in the room, it would be too late.

She would be far gone from there.

All she had was her backpack and her courage.

Everything she had was there.

She would be long gone.

They would never find her.

It was a good thing her name was common. The last time she checked, there must be over one million people named Mary in the U.S. They would never find her. And her looks were not that distinguished either.

Ironically, she'd always tried to blend in, to fit into a family that never really wanted her, or a society that didn't care about people like her. And that was to her advantage as it turned out. She knew that now but she didn't know that back then.

She had to run far away and as fast as she could. She was done with her old life. Everybody knew about her now. She'd been marred by her reputation as a thief, a child stealer, a liar...

Those labels would not apply to her now.

Never again.

She was going to be someone else. She was going to move away and get married and have a family of her own. And she was never going to speak about her past. Ever.

As she continued to walk across the field filled with autumn leaves scattered about the land and trees with almost bare branches, she looked over her shoulder, glancing around in every direction, making sure no one saw her leave.

Her rich, snobby, cruel parents would never know what happened to her now.

It was their fault she was there at the facility being bullied by the staff and other residents. It was all their fault. They just couldn't deal with her. She was a casualty in their little image scam. Nothing more. They never treated her like their daughter. They never tried to get her real help.

Well now, when they find out she'd left the prison they'd placed her into, they would wish they'd never emotionally tormented her or her harassed her. They would be sorry they made her feel as if she was never good enough for them or their perfect little unrealistic world.

Oh, they'd be worried about their reputation, their public image, but Mary didn't care about that right now. That was their problem, not hers. She was free from their lies, from their torment, from their control, their coldness. She was finally free.

They would never find her ever again.

They would never hurt her ever again.

No one would know her little secret.

No one would know about her problem.

And if they did find out about her problem...she would deal with them, just as she'd dealt with everyone else who betrayed her and tried to keep her down. She would destroy them.

Chapter 26 – The Present

Disappointment flooded Caitlyn's veins as she stood in her bedroom. She finished scrolling down her phone ferociously, hoping, praying for a clue.

Nothing.

She received countless text messages, too many to read. She only scanned the previews of each message and many were the same, including:

Oh, Caitlyn. I'm so sorry to hear Katie's missing. Praying she'll be found soon.

Oh, no. Call me. Please let me know if there's anything I can do.

Sorry to hear Katie's gone. Hope they find her soon..

Is it true? Is Katie missing? What happened?

Katie is gone?

Then she saw messages with just emoticons, that's what everyone called them but the actual term was emotion icons. Her contacts were trying to display their emotions through the phone app. She saw many in her texts including:

A sad face emoticon

A pondering face emoticon

A tear emoticon

Wearily, she exited out of the messaging app then threw the phone down on the bed.

There was no hint or clues of anyone taking her daughter. But she knew someone did. Katie didn't just wander away, despite what others think.

She then walked into Katie's room as if hoping she would be there by miracle.

Katie was gone.

Her pretty pink bedsheets still neatly made as Caitlyn had made them this morning. Still untouched from early today.

Her bookshelves filled with her favorite toys.

Caitlyn walked over to Katie's pink toy bin and reached in and pulled out her favorite plush toy and held it to her chest, her heart pounding forcefully. She closed her eyes, hoping for answers, hoping she could see her daughter soon.

Her mind then ran over the events of the early evening when the police questioned everyone. After they were finished with their interrogations in the grand study, Alex, the chef, had come over to her and Sam to say how sorry he was that Katie was missing.

She really appreciated that. But he was the only one. Why didn't the other staff members say anything? Sure, they spoke to their boss, Elaine, to tell *her* how sorry they were that her granddaughter was missing, but what about Katie's parents? Maybe Caitlyn was reading into it too much. Maybe her mind was playing tricks on her. Sometimes people just didn't know what to say. She could tell by reading each of the faces, that they seemed genuinely concerned.

She closed her eyes, breathing hard and fast, feeling as if a panic attack would come on any moment. She was dying inside. Dying to see her daughter again.

She then felt arms around her and shivered momentarily. Sam's aftershave wafted to her nostrils.

"I want our daughter back," she sobbed.

He leaned his head over hers. "I know. I do too."

She could inhale not just his aftershave now, but the scent of beer.

He'd been drinking again.

She wanted to ask how many beers he'd had but didn't bother. He was frustrated and anxious as she was. It was his coping mechanism. She just didn't want him to go overboard and have more than he could handle.

"You know the detective asked us to let him know if anyone gets in touch with us," Caitlyn said, sobbing.

"I know."

"Have you ever wondered why no one has tried to contact us regarding a ransom?"

"Because we're broke?"

"No." She turned to face him. Was he serious? "We might not have much money right now, but your parents sure do."

He sighed heavily. He *was* drunk. Shit.

"Okay, tell me why," he said, wearily.

"Sam, what is wrong with you?"

"What's wrong with me? We've lost our daughter and you're bitching like it doesn't affect me too."

"I didn't say that."

He combed his fingers through his hair over and over again. He was filled with rage. She could tell. He always did that when he was getting crazy about something.

"Listen, please let's not fight. Okay? We've got to pull ourselves together for Katie's sake. Whoever's done this..."

"No one's done this. She ran away."

"What? But earlier you were agreeing with me that she could have been kidnapped."

"By whom? Who kidnapped Katie? Why would they do this?"

She gazed up at him, tears in her eyes. She didn't know what to think right now. But she was not going to give into the heat of the moment. She needed to keep her head straight. At least one of them was sober. Katie, wherever she was right now, needed her parents right now.

She sucked in a deep breath and sighed. "I know our daughter was kidnapped," she said calmly. "And I don't think we're going to be contacted by the kidnapper."

"Why?"

"Because they don't need anything from you or me or your parents." A sick feeling slid into her gut as she continued to speak, her hoarse voice barely a whisper. "They've already got what they wanted."

Chapter 27 – The Present

Later, after Sam went out for a drive with his friend, determined to comb the streets looking for Katie, Caitlyn sat down by the windowsill in her bedroom looking out into the dark night sky.

Moments earlier Sam and Caitlyn had agreed that at least one of them had to stay home in case the cops came back with more information.

At least he was sensible enough to not drive himself, knowing he'd been drinking. A friend picked him up. Caitlyn would never let him go out and drive after having a drink.

Caitlyn's eyes misted up as she glanced down the street wondering where Katie was right now.

Her phone vibrated again. It was probably Tiff calling again but for some reason she just didn't want to talk to her best friend. Tiff had tried calling a million times. She didn't want to talk to anyone.

The street was dark save for a few lights on at some homes. She narrowed her eyes when she noticed that although the light was off at Steve and Mary's home at number 42 across the street, there was someone standing by the window staring directly at Caitlyn's house.

She squinted her eyes to be sure. Yes, she was right. A woman stood in the window.

Mary. It was Mary across the street. The quiet wife who barely said a word earlier when she came over there.

Caitlyn narrowed her eyes, the heat of fury blazed through her body.

Mary knew something. She must know where Caitlyn's daughter was being kept.

She turned around and made her way across the room. She threw her jacket on over her sweats and grabbed her house keys and purse.

Moments later, she made her way down the steps as fast as she could, her heart pumping hard in her chest. What was she going to do when she got over there? Accuse them of something nefarious? She had no proof they knew anything about Katie's disappearance. All she had was a hunch. What if they called the police on her? What if they accused her of harassing them—at three o'clock in the morning?

She knew it didn't look good but the only thought that obsessed her mind was Katie. Her little three-year-old was out there somewhere and the neighbors were acting pretty suspicious. Sam was right though; Steve and Mary were nowhere near the Reede's mansion. Or were they? How would she know? Hundreds of cars passed by that part of town every minute. It wasn't exactly a secluded area. And besides, those idiots didn't even bother to have working security cameras. What was the point in having them at all?

As she opened the front door to head out, Caitlyn froze. Someone was standing there.

Chapter 28 – The Past

Mary got on the train with her backpack and her hopes. She headed to a small town in the next state over where no one would know anything about her past.

This was it. There was no turning back now.

Sweetness County.

That was the name of the town. A nice cozy quaint middle-sized town where everybody minded their own business. She loved the name of the town. It had a very warm and inviting feel to it. She'd spent time Googling the town to ensure it was the right fit. The crime rate was practically non-existent. There were no dramas or major news events happening there. A perfect place to disappear.

She would be a new person there with a new story, a new past. She would find a nice man and get married and live happily ever after.

A sinking feeling slid into the pit of her stomach.

Could she ever truly have a happily ever after?

She glanced around at all the faces on the train, everybody had their eyes glued to their cell phone, scrolling, looking at stories on their social media newsfeed or maybe checking their text messages.

Then...it dawned on her.

The Internet.

What if her past was already posted online? What if a news story came out about her? Her kleptomaniac past. Her crazy parents and their crazy lies about her.

She could hear the words:

Thief.

Klepto.
Baby stealer.
Pet stealer.
Delinquent.

Problem child.

Mary had a sick feeling that her new neighbors might find out about her problem. She had a disturbing thought that her past might eventually catch up to her.

Chapter 29 – The Present

"Tiff, what are you doing out here?" Caitlyn asked, shocked. Her heart raced in her chest, thinking it was a total stranger on her porch. It was so dark outside she didn't recognize Tiff had first.

"I'm sorry to scare you, Caitlyn. I tried to call you all night. I was worried about you. You didn't answer any of my calls. Are you all right?"

Caitlyn sighed heavily. "Thanks for your concern, but of course, I'm not all right. Katie is still missing. The police haven't had any leads and..." Caitlyn's voice cracked. She was beginning to fall apart again.

"I'm sorry," Tiff said. "I'm so sorry you're going through all of this. I know Katie will be found soon."

"How do you know that?" Caitlyn sobbed, trying to regain her strength. The two of them stood at the doorway. Caitlyn wasn't about to invite Tiff in right now and she was probably wondering why.

Tiff looked as if she was about to answer when she noticed Caitlyn's jacket and handbag.

"Where are you going at this time?" Tiff asked.

"Out."

"Out? Out where?"

"Never mind where I'm going."

"Sweetie, are you okay?" Tiff asked again. "Let's go inside and talk. You shouldn't be out at this time of night. Besides, Sam's not even here. What if the police come by?"

Startled, Caitlyn narrowed her gaze on her friend. "How did you know Sam's not here?"

Tiff shifted on the spot, hugging herself. "He told me. When I couldn't get a hold of you by phone, I tried his number and...well, he picked up."

"Oh, did he now?" Caitlyn folded her arms across her chest, her tone was flat.

"He said you were in a state, understandably," Tiff continued. "And...he told me he was going out with a friend to look for Katie. He asked if I could come over and keep you company..."

Caitlyn squeezed her eyes shut; emotion filled her body. Why was she attacking her best friend? She was only concerned about her and trying to help out. She was, after all, Katie's godmother. Of course she would want to do something to help out.

"I'm sorry, Tiff," she sighed deeply, overcome with grief. Her daughter was alive. She knew that much but one could feel grief over any loss. Loss of their daughter who was missing, loss of a job, loss of a way of life, loss of control, loss of anything...

And right now, Caitlyn felt just plain loss, hopeless. Her patience waned with each passing minute. It was three o'clock in the morning and her precious little girl was still lost. Out there somewhere, possibly hurt.

"I'm going over to number 42," Caitlyn finally said as she closed the door behind her and pushed herself gently passed her friend who was still frozen the spot outside the front door.

"Why are you going over there, Caitlyn? They're probably asleep, like everyone else. As you should be."

"Oh, please, Tiff. You can't possibly expect me to sleep when my daughter is still missing. I can't even bare to be in the home alone without her."

"I know, hun. I can just imagine how you must feel, but why are you going over there? Look, see," Tiff said pointing to number 42. "The lights are all off in the house. They're all asleep."

"No, they're not. I saw Mary standing at the window upstairs looking over here as if she's guilty of something. I think she knows where my daughter is," Caitlyn said as she walked briskly across the street. Tiff followed closely beside her.

"Caitlyn," she warned, "Please don't do anything you'll regret. You'll only make this harder on yourself. She's not there."

"How do you know that?"

When they arrived on the doorstep, Caitlyn looked up again at the window. There was no one there. Was it her imagination?

Was she imagining seeing Mary at the window staring out at her? Was Caitlyn going crazy out of her mind over her missing daughter?

She paused for a moment.

"Caitlyn, please, let's just go back to your home. Sam should be back soon."

She turned to go back and then she caught a glimpse the curtains pulling from upstairs. She turned around. Mary was staring down back at her.

"Jeez," Tiff said, also looking up. "Creeped me out. Maybe she heard us."

"No, I don't think so," Caitlyn said, defiantly. She rushed back up the steps and knocked hard on the door.

"Caitlyn, what are you doing?"

"Trying to find my daughter."

She knocked again; this time harder.

She saw the passage light turn on in the house.

A figure of a man in his robe rushed downstairs, taking what looked like angry steps. It was Steve. Caitlyn's stomach clenched into knots. It was too late to turn back now.

Chapter 30 – The Present

"What the hell are you doing?" Steve stuttered as she shouted at her. He looked from Caitlyn to Tiff.

"I'm sorry, but I need to speak with Mary."

"What? Why?"

"I think she might know where Katie is."

His eyes hardened. "Look, I'm sorry your daughter is missing but my wife knows nothing about it."

"I need to speak with her, please." Caitlyn's voice cracked with emotion.

"She's not here. She went to her mother's house."

"What?"

"Good night," he said, closing the door.

Caitlyn put her foot in the door so it wouldn't close in.

"The hell are you doing?" he shouted.

"You're lying. She's here. Is my daughter here too? Are you hiding her here? What have I ever done to you?"

"Besides stealing my watch?" he growled, his eyes challenged her.

"What's going on? What is he talking about, Caitlyn?" Tiff asked, puzzled.

Caitlyn said nothing, she just gazed in his eyes, scoffing, shaking her head. "That's not fair. I gave it back to you."

"So that makes it right? One of us steals things and it's not me, now if you don't leave. I'll call the cops." His tone was hard like his gaze.

She wanted to plead with him to beg him to let her go upstairs to talk to his wife, to find her daughter Katie.

"You can't do this, I just want my daughter back, please."

"I already told you. She's not here."

The lights went on at the neighbor's house next door to his.

He sighed heavily. "Great. You're waking up the whole bloody street. Are you happy?"

"Look, she's just lost her daughter. Cut her some slack. She'll be leaving soon but don't lie to us. We saw your wife upstairs looking out the window."

"She's not here." He slammed the door shut in her face after she moved her foot from blocking the door.

Anger flared through her body. Her blood boiled with fury.

"He can't get away with this. He can't..." Caitlyn sobbed.

She turned around to leave. She then stood at the front of his yard, helpless.

Tiff gave her shoulder a good squeeze. "I'm sorry this happened to you, Caitlyn. Maybe you should just call the detective and tell her what happened but leave it to the cops. They'll find Katie."

Caitlyn didn't catch everything her friend was telling her because her gaze was fixed on something else.

"Caitlyn? You okay? What are you staring at?"

Caitlyn walked over to the garbage bin left out on their yard for garbage pickup. But that's strange. It was Sunday morning. Garbage collection never came on a Sunday.

It was then she noticed something peeking out from the lid.

She walked over to it and pulled it out.

Tiff gasped.

Caitlyn's breath caught in her throat; her eyes widened in horror.

It was a little girl's bright yellow raincoat. It was her daughter Katie's raincoat in the garbage bin in front of her neighbor's home.

Chapter 31 – The Present

Moments later, police and detectives were at the home at number 42. Caitlyn had called the detective as soon as she had the yellow coat in her hands. She also managed to get a hold of Sam who came right back and was at her side, holding her.

The police had come and searched the neighbor's home and sure enough, Steve had told the truth that his wife Mary wasn't home. But the woman Caitlyn and Tiff saw at the window was a maid who'd come to help him clean out the home. It looked as if his wife really was at her mother's home. He'd told the police they had a fight and she'd left.

"No sign of your daughter being in the home, Caitlyn," Detective Smith said.

"But what about my daughter's yellow raincoat?" Caitlyn said, anxiously. She wanted to continue to hug the coat close to her, but the officers said it was evidence.

They would probably check it for DNA.

So her daughter was without a coat? Caitlyn hoped she would at least be inside warm and safe somewhere.

"Who the hell would do this?" Sam said, bitterly.

"I hate to say this but if they were hiding your daughter, it's not likely they would put out the garbage can on a weekend when there's no garbage pick-up and then have the bright coat hanging out where everyone could see it," the detective said.

Caitlyn sighed. The detective was right. It would be conspicuous. It looked as if someone planted it there but who? And why?

Her heart sank.

She was no closer to finding Katie and it was now four o'clock in the morning. Her stomach tightened. She wanted to throw up. She could feel heat rise in her chest.

Katie was still missing and they had no idea where she was.

"We are taking the raincoat in for analysis. This is good that we have something. So far there doesn't seem to be any signs of trauma. Looked as if the coat was taken off neatly. No..."

"No blood, you mean," Caitlyn said.

"Yes. That's right."

"Please let us know if you hear anything," Sam pleaded.

"Yes, we will and we ask that you tell us the same. Thanks for getting in touch with me about the coat," Detective Smith said.

Caitlyn swallowed hard.

Tiff was off to the side and folded her arms across her chest watching everything.

After they'd reached back home, Tiff said, "Do you want me to stay?"

"No, it's all right," Sam said.

"Thanks for coming over," Caitlyn said.

Right now, Caitlyn was spent and still no further to finding her daughter, but they found her coat. At least she thought it was Katie's coat. What if this was just a wild goose chase? Why was the possible kidnapper playing games with Caitlyn?

Chapter 32 – The Present

It was already seven o'clock in the morning and neither Sam nor Caitlyn slept. How could they close their eyes when their three-year-old was still missing?

Sam had already called into work to let them know he would not be coming in and they understood and told him to take as much time as he needed.

Caitlyn had done the same. Most of her clients were very understanding and wanted to help and had already shared a post on their social media pages along with a photo of Katie.

Her stomach lurched thinking about it. What if Katie's parents saw that? What if they were the ones who took Katie? But they had neglected her in the first place. They were not good parents.

She sat in the kitchen getting coffee, Sam was out cold on the couch. It looked as if the beer finally caught up with him. She let him sleep. There was nothing else they could do now but wait.

Just then her phone pinged with an incoming message. It was a photo of Katie grinning in a photo with a piece of cake in her hand.

Caitlyn's heart leaped in her chest; joy bubbled up inside her. A fresh energy filled her.

Katie!

Katie was all right. Her little girl looked happy.

Oh, thank God, Katie was all right—at least in the photo. She wore the same dress she had on early on Saturday and the same hair style. Her hair in two pony tales with her pink clips.

Katie is fine.

I know your secret.

Do not tell the police.

If you want to see her again, meet me at this address.

Come alone.

Come alone or the deal is off...

s

Chapter 33 – The Present

Caitlyn drove along the country road to the location in the message, her heart pumping hard and fast in her chest, a mixture of happiness and fear coursed through her. She was going to finally see her little girl again and hold her in her arms.

Deep down, Caitlyn knew she should have alerted the police or Sam first before responding to the message but she had to see her daughter.

Katie.

She had to see her precious baby girl. Her eyes watered with emotion and determination. She had to see her daughter. The daughter she'd raised since she was a few weeks old.

So the person who took Katie from Caitlyn finally got in touch with her.

How did they even know where to find Caitlyn and Katie? How did they know?

They knew Caitlyn's secret.

The secret that she never wanted to tell anyone.

The horrible secret.

But none of that mattered now. She would get to see her three-year-old daughter Katie again. Finally.

When she pulled up at the old abandoned-looking house, her stomach fell.

Why on earth would they keep Katie there? She hoped to God the house was much nicer on the inside than on the outside.

When she stepped out of her vehicle, she felt a blow to the back of her head then she was out like a light.

Chapter 34 – The Present

Caitlyn's head still hurt as she pried her eyes open slowly. "Where am I? Katie? Where's my baby girl?"

"I'm sorry. I'm so sorry," the voice said. "I had to do this; you understand."

She looked up, her hands were free, thankfully when she opened her eyes and her vision cleared, she could see a woman standing in front of her.

"What? *You?*" Disbelief flooded through Caitlyn. "*You* stole my daughter?"

Chapter 35 – The Past

When Mary got off the train to Sweetness County, her bag and all its contents fell on the pavement. Before long, she inhaled the scent of sweet cologne as she reached to pick her things up...a nice gentleman helped her pick them up.

"You okay, Ma'am?" he said.

His skin was soft and his eyes looked kind and caring. He was handsome in every sense of the word but could she trust him? Could she be that new woman she always wanted to be and start a new life with him? This was called kismet. Sometimes you just know when you meet your soul mate. And he called her Ma'am. He didn't even know her age or how young she was. True, she looked very mature for her age. Everyone always told her that. She would have to get fake ID and make sure everyone thought she was older. Growing up fast meant she was more mature than a lot of people her age, especially after the tough life she'd had to date.

"Yes, I'm fine, thanks."

"Hey, no worries," he said, a boyish grin on his lips. He looked to be around thirty. Yes, that was the age she would choose too. She would tell him she was thirty. She would have to invent a story about her life.

She looked up into his warm brown eyes. He was very handsome. He looked and spoke as if he came from a good background. He was obviously well off. She could just sense these things.

It was then she knew she'd met the man she was going to marry.

Chapter 36 – The Present

Shock filled Caitlyn's body. "Where's my daughter? Where's Katie?"

Her body was numb, she could not believe who was in front of her.

"I don't have her but I know where she is," Lynn, Elaine's housekeeper said. The housekeeper who took Katie's jacket when they first reached the Reede's mansion. She then gave her back the jacket when Katie went outside to play.

A sick feeling slid into Caitlyn's body. "If you've done anything to her, I will..."

"She's okay, Ma'am. She's fine."

"What have you done with her? Where is she?" Caitlyn raised her voice again, panic swirled through her body.

Was this at trick? Did she lure Caitlyn here under pretense? But what about the photo of Katie. Had that photo been doctored?

Lynn looked nervous as she trembled.

"Oh, Ma'am, I made a big mistake. A big mistake."

I'll say.

"What are you talking about?" Caitlyn got up slowly, her head still pounding like a base drum.

"I took Katie, but only for a little while."

"What? Why? You're supposed to be her grandmother's housekeeper. Is this about a ransom. You need a raise so you took her granddaughter for ransom."

Lynn looked around nervously as if expecting anyone to come and find them soon.

"She double crossed me. She was supposed to help me save my house. She promised if I get the kid, she will give me money to save my house and to pay for my mother's medical bills. But she lied. She told me I would get it some other time. The deal was that she was going to give me the money yesterday when I gave her Katie."

Acid burned through Caitlyn's veins; disgust filled her throat as she stared at the woman before her. Contempt flooded through her. The woman pawned off her little girl like she was some old piece of jewelry. Not even giving it another thought? She was her mother-in-law's trusted housekeeper. How could she do this?

"Who was supposed to give you money?" Caitlyn asked, desperate for answers while she bought time figuring out what move to make next. She didn't know if Lynn was going to let her out of there, but she had to get out and get her daughter, to let the cops know where she was, to reach Sam.

"Listen, it's a long story, but...I realize now it was a mistake making a deal with the devil." Lynn walked over to the window and peeked outside through the heavy velvet drapes.

"Tell me what's going on!" Desperation filled Caitlyn's voice now.

There was no way she could remain calm when her daughter was probably stuck somewhere with some nut.

"You see, you don't remember me," Lynn continued talking.

"Remember you? From where? You said you know my secret. What secret is that?"

"I was a maid for the Jacksons."

"The Jacksons?" Caitlyn froze. The name sounded very familiar. A lump climbed in her throat; her spine prickled with heat.

The Jacksons were friends of...her parents.

"No," Caitlyn whispered, breathless, her eyes widened in shock. "No, please no."

"Yes, Ma'am. I know what happened that night."

A flashback whisked across Caitlyn's mind. Fury swirled through her body. The night she wanted to forget. She was locked up in a room in a house in the middle of nowhere. An embarrassment to her family.

They were ashamed of her. They wanted her to be somewhere else but with them.

"Your parents told everyone you went off to some boarding school in Switzerland but you were right here in the States. You were a teenager having a baby."

Caitlyn swallowed hard, remembering when she was seventeen. She shook her head at the memory, tears in her eyes. "No," she whispered again, her voice hoarse.

"The Jacksons said they would take your baby and pretend it's their own."

"And Sheena *is* our baby," another voice came from behind. It was Sue Ellen Jackson. Caitlyn remembered her very clearly now. It was as if that repressed memory was coming back like a flood.

Caitlyn tasted bile in her mouth.

She only just noticed Sue Ellen had a gun in her hand. She then pointed the gun at Lynn and told her to go over to the corner by Caitlyn.

"You double-crosser," Sue Ellen said. "Two-timer. When you worked for me all those years ago, we gave you everything. Now my husband is gone and I have nothing left. You didn't even want to stay with me."

"I had to leave, I'm sorry," Lynn said, sobbing. "The Reedes offered me a great job so I can be..."

"Shut up!" Sue Ellen said.

"And you?" Sue Ellen said, pointing the gun to Caitlyn now. "What are you calling yourself now? Caitlyn. Stupid girl. You think you could just take my child and I wouldn't come looking for you? I knew we had to be careful but I hired a detective and it took all the money we had. Mary Caitlyn Mandeesons. Ha. You thought you could hide by using your middle name? And then you ran off and got married. I bet your husband doesn't know about your past?"

"He will soon."

"Ha! When? After you're dead?"

"I can't believe you would do this. You never deserved Katie."

"Yes, I do. I did. When our daughter died at our home, the authorities said it was on purpose and neglect. That wasn't true. We loved her. They said they'd take any other child we had into children's services. I couldn't believe it. Then I found out we couldn't have any more kids. Your parents were so giving."

"Because you gave them a lot in donations to my dad's campaign. My father cared more about his public image than his family."

"Yes, you knew that, didn't you? It wasn't going to do him any favors preaching about good wholesome family values when he had a thieving daughter and one who got pregnant at seventeen and unmarried. Ha! What a laugh. Good thing he sent you away to have your baby before you started showing. You did it on purpose, didn't you? You always hated them."

"No, I didn't. They were emotionally abusive but...I never hated them. I just hated how they behaved towards me."

"You didn't even come to your parents' funeral. What kind of daughter are you? No wonder they never liked you."

The words cut into Caitlyn like shards of sharp glass.

"That's not fair," Caitlyn said. "I want Katie back."

"Her name is Sheena and she is our daughter. Your parents gave her to us. We adopted her and you stole her from us. A kleptomaniac. That's what you are."

Caitlyn swallowed hard. "So you stole my baby."

"No, we adopted her."

"Without my consent. I had no idea what my parents did. I woke up and the crib was empty. She was a few days old. I..."

"You were mentally ill and still are."

"And you're sane? You've got a gun in your hand. You recruited your former maid to steal back a child that was never yours."

"And she'll never be yours again."

Just then, the door burst open and a man's voice yelled, "Freeze!"

Cops stormed the place and Sue Ellen screamed out in a rage. She finally broke down as they read her rights.

In all of this Sue Ellen and the nervous housekeeper Lynn never asked Caitlyn for her phone. They didn't realize, thank God, that she'd dialed 9-1-1 and had the operators listening this whole time. Everything was now on record.

Chapter 37 – One year later

"Your Halloween costume looks amazing, sweetie," Caitlyn said to Katie as she and Sam sat at a table in the Party Place Restaurant. They were about to go Trick or Treating but decided to treat Katie to a nice family fun Halloween-themed dinner.

Katie's cheeks were painted a beautiful rosy red. Her hair spiraled down like angelic curls. Warmth crept into Caitlyn's body.

"Thanks, Mommy," Katie said, excitedly as she ran her hands over her lovely Princess dress complete with a tiara. She also wore a matching little bag.

Sam and Caitlyn were dressed as Frankenstein and the Bride of Frankenstein.

Katie munched happily on her slice of pepperoni pizza, her favorite food.

Family time.

That's what they were doing. Spending each blessed moment together and celebrating every single holiday and celebration together as a family.

Caitlyn had cut back on her business hours to be there for Katie and her husband. And Sam was now working from home too in his own endeavors to be closer to the family. No more late nights or working weekends for someone else's business.

Caitlyn's heart melted with joy, she was overcome with emotion as her little family listened to the *Monster Mash* song playing over the speakers while laughing and having fun. The mood in the restaurant was cheerful too.

Before today, Caitlyn had always avoided restaurants because of what happened years ago but not anymore. She had been going to therapy and learning how to cope with her emotions. She no longer had the urge to steal—anything.

It was as if facing her fears and her past head on and dealing with the suppressed emotions cured her.

Her therapist had told her the reason she started stealing was because her folks would take things from her, her possessions, her diary notes, her house keys to keep her under control. She had lashed out by stealing after that. But then they took the ultimate thing from her—Katie, her baby girl. That had been the last straw.

She reached over to Katie and gave her a huge squeeze and a hug. Katie hugged her back lovingly.

"Oh, I don't want to squish my brother," Katie said.

Sam hugged Caitlyn's shoulder and hugged Katie. It was the three of them now, soon to be four in their growing family. She was now five months pregnant with her son.

The events of the last year almost faded now as they'd managed to move on from that horrible incident last year.

Detective Smith's words still resonated with her. *"We know who you are. You're Mary Caitlyn Mandeesons. We know all about you. We've been looking you up for a while and knew about the illegal adoption of your baby. Someone had also tipped us off that you were Katie's real mother...we were looking into all angles."*

She was grateful they were on her side and knew that she didn't break any laws but she should have gotten the law involved much sooner instead of taking the law into her own hands by taking her baby back. Why did she do it? She was already undergoing treatment.

Her counselor had tried to grab her when she wanted to leave the facility many years ago. She'd pulled away from him and he fell back and hit his head. Then she left. She never did check to see if he was okay. Turned out he'd had a minor bruise and told the authorities Caitlyn didn't do anything wrong and she was free to leave.

In her mind, her life seemed more interesting when she misremembered the events of her life. She was the one to seek help after her parents locked her away somewhere to have her baby. She wanted to help herself. But then she wanted to leave town.

Sam had heard about Caitlyn's story now. The whole story. She was so glad that he didn't judge her for it.

Elaine had been so apologetic and caring over the past year. She'd blamed herself for not looking out for her family more. Obviously Lynn was arrested for kidnapping and was behind bars awaiting trial.

Sue Ellen was also behind bars. Her husband James had left her after they'd had money problems. He was later found dead in a hotel room. They'd lost their mansion and most of their friends. She kept obsessing of the daughter she wished she had, her second chance as she'd called it when Caitlyn's parents told Sue Ellen about their dilemma and the threat to their public image.

It all fell apart for all of them. Yes, Mary Caitlyn changed her name to Caitlyn and made a move to Sweetness County. She'd told the nice man she'd met that she was going back to her hometown for her little baby girl. She wasn't lying actually. She'd gone back to get her daughter back. The Jacksons used to own a restaurant and bar that had now closed down. Caitlyn never stopped obsessing over her baby girl.

At that time, she had planned to get her daughter back somehow.

They'd left Katie unattended at their restaurant and that was Caitlyn's opportunity to get her back. It worked like a charm. She'd borrowed Sam's car at the time.

They later got married and everything was fine. She never did tell him about her real age in case he looked up her past.

Her folks had died in a private plane crash and she didn't want to go to the funeral knowing the Jacksons would probably attend.

Tiff met someone else now. Tiff and Sam had come clean about their relationship

They'd both gave up a kid for adoption when they were much younger and had met at a support group. They didn't want to reveal they had that in common until much later when Caitlyn confronted their private talks.

It all made sense when Caitlyn thought about it.

Mary and Steve across the street were no longer a couple. They'd had a fight because she caught her husband with the maid. That was another story. And Caitlyn wasn't bothered by it as she and her family now lived in a much nicer neighborhood.

She gave her family a good hug again as they sat in the restaurant ready to have a delicious pizza together and enjoy their happily ever after.

Epilogue

I watch as Mary Caitlyn, her husband Sam, and their little daughter Katie sit down in the restaurant and eat their dinner.

They all look so happy like a nice cozy all-American family spending time together in their Halloween costumes.

I wish I could join them. But they wouldn't want me anywhere near them, not in this lifetime.

I wonder where I went wrong. I am Mary Caitlyn's mother.

Yes, I am still alive. I just had to get away from her father. He died alone in the plane crash. The other body was his mistress. It was impossible to do a DNA test with the ashes after the private plane burst into flames.

I was never on that plane, of course.

I owe my daughter so much. That night, one year ago, I was going to reveal myself to her as I watched her house from the street.

But then...

I lost my nerve.

Would she ever forgive me for the past?

I sigh as I continue to watch them surreptitiously from outside the restaurant window. I had followed them here.

I hate to complicate their life now or burst their happy little bubble of excitement but I would love to meet my little granddaughter, the granddaughter my husband so carelessly gave away because he was worried about his stupid public image. His term never lasted. He'd been caught having an affair with his assistant.

That's why I had to get rid of him.

He'd gotten away with so much in his life. He was an emotionally abusive husband and father, and I regret not being strong enough then to walk away, to take my daughter and run. But he left me anyway and that had been the last straw.

He used to laugh and say he could sell any bullshit story to the world and they'd buy it. I bought his story once. He pretended to be a doting father, a doting husband, an honest local politician.

And now...he's dead.

And all his secrets buried with him.

Well, who is having the last laugh now?

***

Thank you for reading this latest psychological thriller by Ann-Marie Richards. If you enjoyed this book, please leave a review so that other readers could also enjoy their next read.

Books by Ann-Marie Richards

Missing Series – A collection of gripping psychological thrillers

Missing (A gripping psychological thriller with a shocking twist you won't see coming)

Missing Daughter (A gripping psychological thriller with a shocking twist)

She's Missing (A gripping psychological thriller with a shocking twist)

Domestic Psychological thriller series

The Rich Housewife (A gripping psychological thriller with a shocking twist)

The Pretend Wife (A gripping psychological thriller with a shocking twist)

About the author

Ann-Marie Richards has a degree in Psychology and enjoys reading and writing about matters pertaining to the human spirit. She loves to read mild psychological thrillers with a twist, powerful love stories, romance and mysteries. She is thrilled to hear from readers. You can send her an email at annmarierichards.author@gmail.com